DEVIL IN A FRENCH PRESS

ORCHARD HOLLOW  4

A.N. SAGE

CONTENTS

CHAPTER 1

There is a serene quality to living in a small town, especially one that is as hard to find as Orchard Hollow. The air carries a hint of salt from the sea; the smiles are always genuine, and the magical beings running amuck stay secret. At least that was my impression of our quaint residence until my mother showed up on my doorstep after being gone for over a decade.

The thing about Sylvie Addison was that her absence from my life has been both a curse and a blessing. My mom was never the motherly type and when she left, Gran picked up where she dropped the ball. Don't get me wrong, I would never trade the time I spent with my grandmother living in her adorable farmhouse— that I later inherited — for anything. But being left by my wayward mother to figure out life, and magic, on my own kind of stung.

Especially since I recently discovered that I might not be a witch like I always thought but have remnants of Hades' magic coursing through my veins.

That's right, folks! Mother dearest forgot to mention that she may have gotten it on with a descendant of the ancient deity, which resulted in my weirdo powers. Or that she and Gran bound those powers when I was little for reasons I am yet to understand.

All in all, opening the door to see Sylvie with her mane of unruly red hair— one thing we actually had in common— on my porch minutes before my boyfriend came to pick me up for a date was the shock of a lifetime.

"Well, look at what the cat dragged in," Stella Rutherford, my ghost familiar, said from her spot reclining on the sofa. She was almost fully solid today which was a sure way to tell the ghost was in a good mood. The more transparent her gray skin became, the more I knew to stay away. Nothing good came from taking on Stella when she was having a bad day. I learned that from experience. "Or the raccoon, in this case."

My eyes flitted to Harry Houdini's chubby body circling my mom's legs, and I stifled a laugh. Between my ghost familiar's attitude and the wild animal I had unintentionally adopted, the farmhouse was a zoo. Judging by my mom's confused expression, she agreed.

Carefully, Sylvie raised a slender leg and stepped over the raccoon, who proceeded to follow her movement without interruption. Her hazel eyes narrowed in frustration and she flicked her sharp nose in my direction. "Um, honey? A little help?"

I rolled my eyes and reached for the broom I kept near the door. A handy tool when living with Harry Houdini.

"Get off her, you little rascal. Or no treats," I said between clenched teeth as I knocked the broom on the hardwood floor.

The raccoon froze mid-step, the word "treats" having the exact effect I assumed it would. His sharp teeth chattered, and he hissed as he broke away from my mother and darted into the kitchen with more speed than an animal his size should have. I heard the clamor of cupboards being opened, followed by the unmistakable sound of Harry chewing. "That should keep him busy for a while."

Another cupboard slammed. On the sofa, Stella reached her ghostly hand for a slipper I left behind and, after much concentration, chucked it in the raccoon's general direction. Her long ponytail swung over her chest and she stroked the ends with her fingers, smoothing out pretend split ends. As if the woman was ever anything but put together, in life and in death. The slipper flew across the room, landing with a thud not far from the raccoon. My mother's face paled until she resembled a ghost herself. Her eyes darted around the room as she searched for the whoever threw the shoe, having zero luck. Obviously. I was the only one in the family unlucky enough to see the snobby woman.

"Honey, I know it's been a minute," Mom said, her voice trembling, "but what kind of operation are you running here, exactly?"

Leave it to my mom to assume what I had going on was some sort of scam. It was moments like this that reminded me why we never had a close relationship, even when she was around. I shooed Stella away with my hand and walked toward the kitchen to peer over the counter. Harry had snuck off, leaving a trail of open candy wrappers in his wake. Relief flooded through me to know that I didn't have to worry about him destroying the house in the foreseeable future. The raccoon was always his calmest after a sugary snack.

I picked up the wrappers and threw them in the garbage, turning my attention back to the woman in my living room. "Not an operation," I told my mom. "That was Stella Rutherford, my ghost familiar. The one I told you about multiple times on our last call. Which was months ago, by the way. Thanks for checking in."

"Right, well, no matter. More important things at hand."

The important thing she was referencing was the doomsday message she came to deliver and the reason I was stuck at home on a Friday night and not out with Joe canoodling in a cozy restaurant. Gran was right—life was a witch and then you died.

I sighed, gulping the cold coffee sitting in a mug on the counter. The logo of my cafe, Bean Me Up, had scratched off the front, but seeing a piece of it made me feel warm and fuzzy inside. Even with my mom's chaos unfolding before me, there were some things that couldn't be destroyed. I peered at my familiar and the faces she was making behind Sylvie's back, snickering. I had Stella, Joe, and my cafe. Life was good; I simply had to keep reminding myself of that.

"Not that I'm not glad to see you again," I told my mom in an attempt to keep the peace, "but you said there was an emergency."

Sylvie's face darkened. "I said your life is in danger, as is the entire world."

"Ominous," Stella mused. "I'll leave you two to it. Catch me up when you're all done here."

With that, my familiar vanished into thin air,

leaving me alone with the hot mess express train that was my mother. So much for solidarity between a witch and her ghost bestie. I shook my head, pulling out a bar stool to perch on while I attempted to get to the bottom of why my mom showed out of the blue.

"What does that mean, Mom?" I pressed. "You've said it twice already, and I'm as lost now as I was when you arrived. I canceled a date for this, so if it's another one of your theatrics—"

Sylvie held her hand up to my face, cutting me off. "You are exactly like your grandmother," she said with a sigh. "Always looking for the dark cloud in a situation."

This coming from the woman who just told me the world might end... I grimaced.

"I don't want to get in the middle of whatever issues you and Gran had," I told her. "Can you please tell me what the danger is so I can figure out what to do about it?"

There was no nice way to say it but the truth of it was, even if I did know what dangers lurked in the shadows, there was little I could do to help. My witch powers never came through properly and at this point, I doubted they ever would. Every spell I tried had backfired, some quite literally, and if I were to try a protection spell, I'd likely burn the house down. Mom, on the other hand, was a powerful Addison witch.

Some said even more powerful than Gran, and that woman was the strongest paranormal I knew. Which was why I was incredibly confused when Sylvie came here instead of handling the problem on her own. Surely, if the world was in mortal danger, I was the last person she'd reach out to for help.

I was even more confused about why she was being tight-lipped about it.

"What's going on, Mom?" I asked again.

"Too much to get into tonight," Sylvie replied. "Now, is my room still upstairs, or did your grandmother have it filled with cement to make sure I couldn't move back in?"

I huffed out a frustrated breath, my wild red hair flapping as I did. Before me, my mom's identical mane bounced as she swirled to inspect the farmhouse. "For the millionth time, Gran never wanted you to leave. You did that all on your own."

"So... the room?"

Wincing, I avoided her eyes when I said, "Oh, it's gone. It's a magic items storage area now. But the guest room is made up so you can sleep there."

Sylvie flashed all her teeth, giving me her best told-you-so look. With her coat discarded on the floor by the front door, she looked the picture of the woman who left us so long ago. Curly hair gathered in a messy bun resembling a beehive, a floral dress down past her knees, tall cowboy boots the color of blood, and a silk scarf that wrapped around her neck three times and tied in a loose knot at her chest. I wanted to hug her so badly it hurt.

"I don't know how you live in this stuffy place."

And the urge for physical contact was gone in an instant.

"This stuffy place is my home," I replied, battling the urge to start an argument. "You can have the guest room or you can see if the bed and break-fast has vacancies. Either way, we're having a conversation tomorrow morning, whether you like it or not."

The scolding earned me a theatrical salute. "Aye, aye, captain," my mother said teasingly. "See you in the morning, daughter of mine."

As she sauntered up the stairs, discarding layers of her clothes on the stairs with each passing step, I rubbed my throbbing temples. I could already feel a headache careen from side to side and the evening wasn't even over yet. Picking up what I could after Mom, I piled her clothes on the small table at the front entrance, bundled up in a warm coat, and stepped onto the front porch, closing the door silently behind me.

"Are we all dying or what?"

I jumped. "Jeez, Stella! You did it again!"

"Sorry, sorry," my familiar said, her hands up in surrender. "I'm curious, kill me. Again. Kidding."

My eyes rolled skyward while I crossed the porch to sit on the bench outside. The crisp evening air chilled my cheeks and my lungs burned as I inhaled and exhaled, attempting to meditate the night away. "Still no answers. She said she'll explain tomorrow but I'm not sure how much of that is true."

"Do you think she's right and you're in danger?"

I shrugged.

"Very convincing," Stella said. "You know what this means, don't you? You're going to have to house your mother until the matter is settled. Think you're ready for that?"

"Since when are you concerned about my well-being?"

This time it was the ghost who shrugged. Her slender shoulders hiked up to her ears and when she turned away from me to watch the dark outline of the trees in the distance, I thought I glimpsed the remnants of worry lines around her eyes. Which was impossible given how much money Stella spent on making them line-free when she was alive.

The ghost puffed out her big lips. "I'll give your mother one thing— the woman sure knows how to make an entrance."

"Right? She's so dramatic!"

I imitated my mother walking through the door, and we burst out laughing. Tears stung my eyes; I wiped them away before they froze on my face. Winter was right around the corner and I could already feel the weather shift. While it was great to be hidden between the mountains and the vast sea, it didn't make for the best cold weather. There was one year that we got so much snow people couldn't get out of their house. Gran was always prepared with a spell, but since I was useless on that front, I had to improvise. Luckily, I had Joe this year to help out around the farmhouse if things got rough.

My heart warmed thinking of the vampire I was dating.

"I know that look," Stella said, annoyed. "That's my cue to leave."

Shaking myself back from daydreaming, I watched her sheer body vibrate, then start to disappear. Before she left, Stella re-materialized one more time to say, "Don't forget to keep the back door open for the monster."

"I knew it! Harry is growing on you!" I yelled after her but she was already gone.

Back pressed into the metal of the bench, I wrapped the jacket tighter over my chest and peered into the night. Beyond the farmhouse, the forest stood stoic, a dark stain against an even darker sky. Deep within it, the ley lines powering the magic of the paranormals in our town pulsed under the earth, and beneath them, who knew? More Orchard Hollow secrets, I bet.

I smiled, pulling out my phone to text Joe goodnight. As I did, I looked at the front door, my mood slightly souring at the thought of my mother sleeping inside. Something about her surprising return frustrated me and I couldn't figure out what it was. I should have been pleased, yet I wasn't.

Pushing the thought away, I typed a message and pocketed my phone. What I needed was a glass of wine and a good night's rest. There was nothing I could do this evening and mom's insanity could wait until the morning. I glanced at the vintage watch Gran left me. What could go wrong in ten hours?

CHAPTER 2

"Sylvie Addison? As I live and breathe, I never thought I'd see you here again!"

Dumping the folding sign on the pavement, Ray stretched his beefy arms and pulled my mother in for a hug that lasted forever. His back muscles tensed as he lifted her up, feet dangling a few inches above the ground. I waited for her to try to escape but instead, Mom returned the hug, laughing as Ray swirled her in a circle before putting her down.

"Ray Livington," she said, patting him on the shoulder. "You haven't aged a day."

The ice cream shop owner smiled widely. "Such a flatterer."

Were we talking about the same Sylvie Addison? I didn't remember Mom ever saying anything that wasn't double-edged. In fact, her compliments usually had a second meaning that was more insult than flattery. Whoever this Sylvie was, it wasn't the woman I grew up with.

As we walked down Cliff Row, I was once again reminded of how little I truly knew about my mother. Her entire expression changed with every person we passed, all of whom she seemed to know by name. I had lived in this town for my entire life and I didn't even know half these people. Yet here was Mom, chatting them up like she'd never left. It was unsettling.

"Come in for a scoop," Ray said, gesturing to the display freezer inside his shop. "Rocky Road with chocolate drizzle, if I remember correctly?"

Giggling, Mom elbowed him in the arm playfully. "You have the best memory. We're going to visit Piper's amazing cafe, but I promise to stop in for a scoop soon. Have to get some Rocky Road in me!"

Seriously, who is this woman?

Ray had always been friendly, but I can't remember the last time he offered me a free scoop. I chalked it up to him being a werewolf— they tended to run hot and cold with their emotions— but seeing him light up around my mom made me wonder if I had it all wrong. Not the werewolf part; I was pretty sure I guessed that correctly. Paranormals didn't advertise themselves and most stayed under the radar, even from other magical beings, though with some, it was easier to tell. Werewolves were especially easy to spot on account of their size and all the hair. It helped that Ray wore his family's talisman around his neck like a badge of honor.

A magical talisman was passed down from one generation to the next, often falling to the firstborn in each family. It contained the magic of each family member and helped strengthen the magic of the paranormal wearing it. Having one was a great help for most of us. That is, unless one should happen to break theirs like I did. In my defense, it broke while I was fighting for my life and, as it turned out, the talisman was useless for my brand of non-witch magic, anyway. I missed the brooch I used to wear regularly. So much so that I found myself reaching for my chest where it used to sit every once in a while.

I must have been doing exactly that as we left Ray's shop because Mom asked, "Where's the talisman? You never part with that gaudy thing."

"It broke," I said with a scowl. "Long story."

I knew I'd have to tell her about my extracurricular activities of chasing down killers at some point, but I didn't feel like opening up that can of worms right now. Especially when it seemed everyone came out of the woodwork this morning to say hello. Cliff Row, the main street in our little town, was usually bustling. Between the locals and the tourists, it was hard to get through without bumping at least a couple of shoulders on your way. But the tourist season was winding down, and I assumed it would be an uneventful visit today. A quick pop in at Bean Me Up to show Mom the place and we'd be on our way. At least, that was what I'd told myself this morning.

It definitely was not what happened.

"Sylvie! Over here!"

A high-pitched voice rang out from down the street. I peered around Mom's messy bun to see Nancy Steeles speed-walk toward us, my blood running cold. The last thing I needed was to have another altercation and there was no speaking to Nancy without wanting to slap the woman. Why was she even coming over? She'd made it clear that she couldn't stand me, so why bother sucking up to my mom?

I watched Nancy straighten her fuchsia blazer as though she was entering a job interview. *Ah, of course.* Nancy was one of the town's witches, a fairly competent one at that, and around these parts, Addison witches were basically royalty. Myself excluded on account of not having much magic to show off. Someone like Nancy, who loved to have her nose in all things paranormal, wouldn't miss a chance to chat up the infamous Sylvie Addison. She used to do the same thing with Gran, and it made me sick to my stomach. So much flakiness in one person was uncanny.

High heels clicking on the pavement, Nancy hurried our way, her false smile growing with each step. "I thought that was you. Welcome back, Sylvie!" she said, then looking at me darkly added, "Hey, Piper."

I mumbled a hello, wishing to disappear in the style of my ghost familiar.

"Ah, Nancy Steeles," my mom mused. "How are you and the coven? Seeing anyone special?"

Nancy's cheeks heated, and the color spread down her neck, making her camouflage into her blazer. With her cheeks puffed out while she thought of an answer, she resembled a pink balloon. I couldn't be certain, but I had the inkling that Mom added the dating jab for my benefit. Nancy had it in for me since high school and while I never talked to my mother about my personal problems, it seemed she'd been paying attention after all.

My heart melted a little at the idea.

"N-not anyone special, no," Nancy stuttered. "I'm keeping my options open."

"Well, don't keep them open for too long," Mom warned. "None of us are getting any younger."

If Nancy was pink before, she was the unmistakable shade of a tomato now. "Right. Well, I hope we can get you to stop by a coven meeting some time before you leave. Unless you're back for good?"

"It would be a pleasure," my mother said sweetly. "I'll be in touch."

With that, Mom waved and pulled me along, leaving Nancy in the dust with her mouth gaping open. I looked over my shoulder, suppressing a smile. "You're not actually going into their lair, are you?" I asked.

"Heavens, no! That girl is insufferable. Now where is this cafe of yours? I could sure use a pick-me-up."

Putting more distance between us and Nancy, we made our way down the street toward Bean Me Up. My steps quickened when we passed Joe's bookshop, for fear he might spot us and decide to step out. As oddly sweet as my mother was acting this morning, I wasn't ready to open that can of worms.

Across the street, the Rose Hollow Hotel blocked out the sun, casting dark shadows over the entire street. I wondered if Cilia was working today and if she was planning to stop by for a coffee, as she often did these days. Despite being in Nancy's coven, Cilia Craven was the only witch in town I considered a friend. Mostly because she kept making me join her for drinks on the weekends. Not that I could complain, it was nice to have another witch to talk to. It was even nicer to get away from Stella's ghostly attitude.

I swung the door to the cafe open and led Mom inside. She scanned the area approvingly, a gleam of excitement sparkling in her hazel eyes. Clapping her hands together, she started for the counter and stopped when she noticed Rory serving a customer his drinks. The teen's space-buns bounced up and down as she worked and she readjusted them periodically, her sparkly blue nail polish glimmering as she did.

"Is that—"

"Rory Craven," I said. "Cilia's niece and my assistant."

Mom's eyes narrowed. "Also a witch."

"How did you know?"

"Honey, please. I know this town inside and out."

While my mother settled into one of the empty tables by the window, I said hello to Rory. The teenager had truly blossomed into her own in recent months. So much so that I had no trouble taking days off without worrying about the espresso machine exploding. It was night and day from her first shift on the job.

Skirting around the counter, I let Rory take the lead at the register and whipped up the drinks for my mother and me. Today, I settled for two Gingerbread Lattes, a new staple at the cafe that I'd added last week in time for the cold season. The lattes were actually Rory's idea, something she thought of when she was babysitting her twin cousins. I had to admit, they were absolutely delicious.

I added a sprinkle of cinnamon to the whipped cream and inhaled the spicy air, passing by Rory on my way to the table. "How was the morning?"

"The usual," the teen witch said. Her fingers threaded through her hair while she typed on her phone. All this in between serving customers; the kid could multitask. "Joe stopped by in the morning."

"Did he get a drink?"

Rory glanced at me briefly, nodded, then went back to her phone. "Not sure why. He can't drink them and not like you were here, anyway."

She had a point. Vampires didn't eat or drink regular food and, though Joe abstained from human blood, he still couldn't exactly down a latte with the rest of us. Most vampires enjoyed the idea of holding a cup or ordering a meal at a restaurant, but that was mostly for show. To better blend in with those around them. Joe had no reason to do so at Bean Me Up; Rory and I both knew what type of paranormal he was.

It was sweet he kept buying drinks to help the cafe though.

"Is your mom staying for long?" Rory asked.

I did a double-take, shocked by her sudden interest in my life. Rory was a damn good witch and, as of recently, a pretty decent assistant, but she was a teenager. There was a limit to how much she cared for the adults around her. I eyed her suspiciously. "I'm not sure," I answered honestly. "Why?"

"Because if she is, you might want to handle whatever that is—" she pointed to the table Mom sat in "—before you're left to deal with the fallout."

Heart pounding in my chest, I looked up and froze. Mom was no longer alone at the table. Standing in front of her with her hands on her hips was none other than Mrs. Cevil, the sweet old lady who ran Bakes and Cakes and the same woman who supplied the goodies I sold at the cafe. From where I stood, it looked as if the two were having a very heated discussion. Right in front of my customers.

I exchanged a look of concern with Rory, picked up the lattes, and stomped over. The whipped cream bounced as I deposited the cups on the table, pretending not to have seen the two arguing before.

"Hello, Mrs. Cevil," I said, sugar dripping off every word. "I didn't realize you knew my mother."

The old woman looked flustered when she saw me. Her hands brushed the floral apron she wore over her pink cardigan, and she continued to rake them over the fabric repeatedly. "Only popping in to welcome Sylvie back to the neighborhood. I should get back to the bakery, it's really getting on."

I sneaked a peek at the spaceship clock above the door. Ten in the morning. *Hmmm.*

"Are you sure you don't want to join us for a drink? I can ask Rory to get another Gingerbread Latte ready for you."

"Piper, honey," Mom interrupted. "Let Reeba go. She's probably very busy running her own business. You know all about that."

Reeba? It was odd to hear Mrs. Cevil's first name on my mother's lips. I had never heard her mention the woman and what I saw before I interrupted certainly looked nothing like the friendly chatter the two were pretending to have right now. Something was going on and, once again, I was being kept out of it. Anger bubbled in my gut and as I said goodbye to Mrs. Cevil and watched her walk out the door, I couldn't help but direct it at my mother.

She sipped on her latte, her smile dropping when she saw my glare. "Go ahead..."

"You said you'll explain why you're here and you are yet to do so. And what were you arguing with Mrs. Cevil about?"

My mother sighed, placing her cup on the table and tapping a red painted fingernail on the glass. She sucked in a long breath, eyeing me carefully. "You're right," she said. "It's time I tell you everything."

CHAPTER 3

Lightning flashed over my fingers as I rolled my magic over my palms, extinguishing it before it escaped. I did this over and over again, my mind reeling. In the background, Rory's music blared while she cleaned up the cafe, ready to close up for the night.

"That's all she told you?" Stella asked. The ghost's face popped into my sightline, making me drop the hold on the lightning.

I pressed my lips into a thin line. "Yep. We were on the right track and my magic is that of Hades. Mom was pretty vague on the details, which, trust me, I'm thankful for."

"So M is Malachi, your Underworld father."

"He's not from the Underworld," I corrected. "His bloodline is connected to the ancient deity. Nothing more."

Stella scoffed, crossing her long legs as she perched on the edge of my desk. My familiar must have had some sort of ghost intuition because she showed up immediately after Mom finished spilling her guts. Since I didn't know what to say to my mother after her revelation, Stella and I snuck off into the cafe's back office to digest what I learned. Which wasn't as much as I'd hoped. Thanks for nothing, Sylvie.

The ghost blew out a whistling breath. "Potato potahtoh. Same difference."

"It's tomato. Who says potahtoh?" I asked. "Anyway, this Malachi character is my father, but Mom said she hadn't spoken to him in years, not since Gran and her bound my dark magic."

"And she didn't say why they did it?"

I shook my head. "Not really. I'm assuming it's because they thought it was dangerous. Mom used the words 'for your own good' repeatedly, so I think she believes they were doing the right thing. Same as when she left."

"To infiltrate the Sisters of the River, the witch coven worshipping Hades?" Stella asked, catching up to the story.

The ache in my temples returned, and I rubbed

them in tiny circles, hoping to stop the oncoming headache. Ever since Mom showed up out of the blue, I'd had a non-stop pressure behind my eyes, making it impossible to think clearly. I took a slow sip of my left-over latte, finding Stella's eyes. "Apparently Gran knew about it all and she asked Mom not to go, that she would be putting all our lives in danger. Didn't stop her from running headfirst into it, though."

"That explains where you get it from."

Insulted, I picked up the stress ball on the desk and tossed it through Stella's chest before she had the chance to blink out of sight. The ghost glitched, grimacing as the ball passed through her body and landed on the other side of the desk with a thump.

"Please," she said. "We both know you're not exactly a 'think first, act later' individual. Why did your mother think the Sisters were up to no good?"

I shrugged my shoulders and leaned back in the office chair, my knees pressing to the edge of the desk and my feet dangling in the air. "This part I didn't quite understand. She was talking in circles. From what I could milk out of her, the Sisters of the River have some strange plan to summon Hades. Mom said they'd been working on it for generations, but some-thing always goes wrong, as though there is a missing ingredient to their spellwork. She mentioned a vessel and a bunch of other things I didn't catch." I sucked in a sharp breath and held it. "It all sounded very out there, to be honest."

To my left, Stella quirked a brow.

"You're right," I said. "Nothing is off the table when it comes to the Addison witches; I should know that by now. Do you truly believe Mom's right?"

"I think that she wouldn't dare show her face back here after being gone for so long if she had another choice," Stella replied. "If your mother is here, trouble is not far behind. At least from what I can gather."

Unfortunately, I agreed with the ghost. Mom was convinced that the Sisters were onto something big, that it could set their entire vicious plan into motion. The only problem was that Sylvie didn't know what it was or why things were different this time around. Whatever the Sisters were planning, it was dire. And according to my mom, it could bring about the end of the world as we know it.

Which made sense because raising an ancient death god probably had some pretty terrible consequences.

Wonderful.

A head popped through the half-open doorway. "Are you decent?" Rory asked, her eyes averted.

"Huh? Of course!" I exclaimed. "Why wouldn't I be?"

"I don't know what you do back here." The

teenager pushed her way through the door, mop in hand. She settled it against the supply shelf and scanned the room. "Mind if I use this place tonight after you lock up?"

I gaped at her questioningly.

"There's a spell I want to try out, but I can't do it at home because my stupid brothers are usually there. They make it impossible to practice, and this is the only place I can think of that has any privacy."

"What kind of spell?" I asked.

Rory flashed her front teeth. "Just an illusion one," she said. "Nothing that goes boom, I promise."

I bit my bottom lip, considering it. Rory has been a great help around the cafe and I'd hate for her not to practice her magic, especially since, from what her aunt told me, she was very capable. And after growing up with a nosy mother, I knew all about needing privacy. While I couldn't let her stay in the cafe all alone at night, I figured there was no harm in giving her some space while I ran errands.

Checking the time on the open laptop in front of me, I closed the lid and said, "Tell you what? I have to go see Mrs. Cevil about tomorrow's order and will be gone for a half hour or so. Is that enough time?"

"Yes! Thank you so much, Piper!" the teen beamed.

As I slinked out through the back door into the

alley, she was already setting up her supplies. I smiled, my chest warming at the sight of the young witch and her excitement. She reminded me a lot of myself. I was equally eager to practice magic when I was Rory's age and Gran encouraged me to keep going. If I could do the same for another witch, I was more than happy to return the favor.

Motioning for Stella to give the girl some privacy, I shut the door behind me and made my way down the alley and toward the main street. Bakes and Cakes, Mrs. Cevil's bakery, was only a block away and if I hurried, I'd catch her before she left.

Above my head, the moon hung low, and its bright light illuminated the quiet street. Most shops had already closed but some worked on finishing off for the day. I waved hello to a few locals as I passed them, hurrying my steps to get out of the cold quicker. When I finally reached the bakery, I felt my entire body exhale. My breath rose before me in a white cloud as I turned the handle and stepped over the threshold.

Eyes adjusting to the low light, I let my gaze drift over the cute shop. Even with most of the ceiling lamps turned off— an easy sign to know Mrs. Cevil was closed for the evening— the bakery was still the most adorable business on Cliff Row. The walls were painted a candy pink and every counter and table was an off-white, giving the shop a dollhouse appearance.

The edges of the rounded display were carved to resemble doilies, adding to the French-country charm the bakery had. There were three round tables lining the large bay window with clear acrylic chairs pulled into them; pink, puffy roses in tiny vases adorned each tabletop. To my right, a large built-in unit spanned the length of one wall, its shelves full of yummy-looking treats all wrapped in pink and tied off with pristine bows.

I heard a clutter in the back room where Mrs. Cevil kept her kitchen and snuck around the corner to get my order in before she left for the night.

As I ducked into the small baking area, the old woman jumped at the sight of me, a tray of muffins wobbling in her hands. "Goodness, Piper! You scared me half to death."

"I'm so sorry, Mrs. Cevil," I said, my cheeks reddening. "I wanted to stop in before you close to put my order in for tomorrow."

The shop owner wiped her brow with the back of her hand, smearing a line of flour across it. I battled the urge to wipe it off.

"What will it be, dear? Two cases of muffins, three of the scones, and a croissant tray?"

My usual. I agreed, adding, "And the huckleberry pie if you have one."

"I don't," Mrs. Cevil said, then glancing at the gold

watch on her wrist, said, "But I suppose I can whip one up for you before I leave."

"Oh, no! Please don't stay late on my account. I can get it next time."

Mrs. Cevil put down the tray and started packaging up the muffins. The smell of apples and oranges lingered in the air; my stomach growled with hungry cries. Embarrassed, I patted the angry beast and smiled sheepishly at the baker, who said, "You're welcome to sit down for one. I can put a tea on for you."

"I wish," I answered. "Rory is alone in the cafe and I shouldn't leave her to her own devices for too long. Plus, I have to get back home in case Mom decides to redecorate."

Eyes narrowing, Mrs. Cevil fidgeted with the ribbon of her apron, her gaze never meeting mine. I got the sense that she wanted to speak but was holding off, briefly wondering if it was about what I saw earlier. She and my mother definitely had something going on, I desperately wanted to get to the bottom of it.

Taking a step in, I ducked my head to catch the old woman's attention. Her gold-rimmed glasses fell down her pointed nose. She pushed them up, tucking a piece of curly gray hair behind her ear before finally looking at me. "What were you and my mom chatting about this afternoon?" I asked.

"Only catching up, dear." The wrinkles covering the woman's face deepened. "You know how it is in this town. When someone leaves and comes back, it makes the news."

"Oh, okay," I said, deflating. "It seemed as though you may have been arguing. I thought I'd make sure everything is fine."

Mrs. Cevil hid from me again, busying with the tray that needed no attention. She packed and repacked the same box until I got the point. *Time to leave, Piper.*

Thanking her for the order and letting her know I'd be by in the morning to pick it up, I left Mrs. Cevil to her muttering and headed for the front. As I stepped out of the kitchen, she called after me. I whipped around, noting the lines of concern around her eyes.

"Do me a favor, dear," she said flatly. "Tell Sylvie I'm glad she returned and that I hope she plans to stay this time. One can't outrun the past; it always comes knocking."

I waited for her to expand. And waited. When Mrs. Cevil turned her back on me to tend to the oven, I realized that was as much as I was going to get out of the woman. Mildly confused, I stumbled out of Bakes and Cakes and wobbled down the street toward the cafe. The warm light of familiar ground beckoned me forward and yet when I stepped inside and heard the bell above the door that usually made me smile, I didn't feel relieved. A foreboding sense of dread gripped my bones, refusing to let me go.

The way Mrs. Cevil spoke about Mom was ominous and distracting. I was getting more of a sense that the two knew each other, and in a much deeper way than either let on.

Speeding to the office to let Rory know I was back, I made a mental note to question Sylvie about it when I got home. This time, I wasn't going to let my mother bulldoze over me. She had better give me a proper explanation, or I was going to send her packing. Family or not, I was done being her fool.

I glowered, remembering Mrs. Cevil's final words. The past sure did latch on, didn't it?

CHAPTER 4

The farmhouse was alive when I finally pulled into the driveway and parked the Beetle. Lights were on in every room of the house and there was music blaring from the wide-open front door. I winced, thinking of the electric bill I would get at the end of the month, thanks to Sylvie's lack of consideration. Slamming the car door louder than I normally would, I stomped up the driveway, my boots kicking pebbles in all directions, and headed straight for the porch.

I froze as soon as I neared it.

It appeared that not only was my mother having herself a fun little party; she wasn't alone.

Blood rushed to my face as I watched Sylvie scoot

closer to Joe, her arm wrapped around his shoulder. Her lips, painted a bright red, were so close to his ear I thought she was going to take a bite out of it. My heart raced while my mom whispered something in my boyfriend's ear, then rolled her head back to laugh. As she did, Joe joined in, his green eyes crinkling at the corners. Mom's barnacles still attached, Joe raked his fingers through his short hair, continuing to chuckle.

What in the name of coffee was going on here?

I cleared my throat, arms crossed tightly at my chest.

"Piper, honey! It's about time you came home!" my mom exclaimed. Unraveling herself from Joe like a python leaving its prey, she jumped off and strolled to the porch railing. I heard the clinking of glass seconds before Sylvie rushed toward me with a bottle of wine in hand. "You work too hard. Have a drink."

The wine was shoved in my hands and my fingers curled around the neck, freezing over it. I noticed no glass was offered, as though my mother wished for me to gobble the wine straight from the bottle. I looked around. Did I step through a wormhole into a dorm party?

Large, warm hands lifted the bottle from me; the smell of peppermint in the air. My knees knocked as Joe's breath brushed over my face. "Hey, you."

"Hi," I choked out. "What are you doing here?"

Joe leaned in closer, his body pressing against mine until there was not an inch of frigid air between us. "I wanted to see how you were holding up," he said. Then, gesturing to my mother who was currently dancing on the porch. "Glad to see everyone is alive."

"Not for long," I joked.

I let Joe guide us to the front porch where Mom's theatrics amplified by a million. She'd somehow managed to find the silk scarves I had put away for donation and was wearing at least seven of them around her, forming a flowing skirt that twirled as she spun in circles. I didn't know what kind of magic was keeping the woman from passing out, but it seemed to go on forever.

After a few minutes of her so-called dancing and Joe and me watching awkwardly, she finally settled down, snatching the bottle from us and pouring a hefty amount into a coffee mug.

Oh, goodie. At least there were mugs involved.

"How long did you have to put up with this?" I whisper-asked Joe.

He chuckled under his breath, not breaking eye contact with me. "Not long. And she's not so bad," he admitted. "I think you two have more in common that you think."

"Blasphemy! You take that back or I'll sic Harry on you." I glanced through the open door, cringing at the messy state of my usually organized home. "Speaking of, it seems Mom managed to chase him and Stella away. I didn't think anyone had that kind of power."

"She *is* an Addison witch," Joe teased.

I curled into him. His chest rose up and down at my back, lulling me into a peaceful state and relaxing my every bone. Eyes closing, I pretended it was only the two of us, on the beach by the sea or in some quaint cottage in the middle of the woods. Some place where there was no phone reception and the closest neighbor couldn't be spotted for miles. Perhaps somewhere in the mountains. It was so peaceful inside my mind that for a moment I almost forgot we weren't alone on the porch.

A silky fabric slapped my cheek, and I jumped, startled.

"I'm going to get a refill," Mom said, waving the empty bottle of wine in my face. "Do you want me to bring you out a mug?"

I shook my head. Suddenly, a thought occurred to me. Sylvie was a bottle deep and definitely relaxed. If I wished to coax answers out of her, now was as good a time as any. I turned around to face Joe and mouthed "go with it" out of Mom's earshot. Twisting back, I grabbed the bottle from Sylvie, placed it on the small iron table near the bench and said, "Come sit for a bit, Joe will get us more drinks."

The vampire arched a bushy brow but didn't complain. Standing, he walked into the house and shut the door behind him, giving us the privacy we needed. Thank goodness for a man who could read between the lines.

"That one is a keeper, honey," Mom said. "Even for a vampire."

"How did you... You know what? Never mind. You're right, he is pretty great."

Sylvie stretched her long legs out, the boots she stole from my closet peeking out from under her makeshift skirt. The way she moved reminded me so much of the carefree woman I loved when I was younger. Back when I admired her wild ways and didn't associate her traits with abandonment. I had to hand it to her, when Mom was in her element, she could take your breath away.

Thinking of her this way made Joe's comment about our similarities sting a little less.

Glancing at the door, I tried to hear inside to gauge how much time I had before Joe returned, but couldn't make out his movements. He was either staying still on purpose or his vampire abilities had kicked in. Either way, I figured I'd better get straight to the point while my mother was in a good mood.

"I saw Mrs. Cevil after work," I blurted out.

Beside me, Sylvie stopped breathing.

"She made it sound like you two know each other quite well," I pressed. "Mentioned the past catching up to you."

"She threatened you?" Mom shrieked.

That took an unexpected turn. Why was that where her mind went? Mom's reaction only confirmed what I already knew; the women were lying to me. I pulled away to see her face better. "Not at all. Tell me the truth, Mom. How do you know Mrs. Cevil?"

The woman who was supposed to be my entire world turned away. Her eyes blinked rapidly and she worked her jaw, the words falling short. She gazed over the porch at the Beetle parked in the driveway as though it held all the answers. A lump formed in my throat and I readied for another rejection.

Instead, my mother sighed, saying, "Do you remember when you got that piece of junk?"

"End of high school," I answered. "You told me I could drive, but I had to get my own car."

Sylvie Addison laughed. "I was hoping you couldn't afford it, so I didn't have to worry about you driving into a tree. But then you showed up here with that thing, your face beaming like you struck gold. You were so happy."

"I wanted to be free."

"You and me both, kid," she whispered. "I know you hate me for leaving, and I don't blame you. There is a lot you don't understand about why I had to go, a lot *I* don't even understand myself. But trust me when I tell you, it was to protect you and Gran. To keep you safe."

Frown lines creased my forehead. "Why, Mom? Why couldn't you tell me the truth about my magic? Why bind it and run away?"

"It's complicated."

"Then tell me! I'm not a kid with a beat-up car in your driveway anymore!" My gaze flicked to the Beetle. Ugh. "Please tell me how you running off to join a dark magic coven was for my own safety, because I don't get it. At all."

Silence enveloped the porch. My mother continued to stare straight ahead, her lips shut tightly. I'd pushed too hard. There was no way she would open up now. I knew it. I bit the inside of my cheek until I tasted iron. "At least tell me about Mrs. Cevil. I work with the woman. I deserve to know if I should be worried."

"You have nothing to fear from Reeba," Mom replied. "She is an ally. Probably the only one we have in this war."

"Are you saying Mrs. Cevil is helping you with the Sisters of the River? Is she a witch?"

Mom nodded slowly.

Holy latte. Consider my mind blown because I

had no clue that Mrs. Cevil was a paranormal, let alone a witch. And I'd spent so much time with her. Stella was right, I really did have a crap nose for all things magic.

"How? What are you two planning?" I asked. "You said the coven is dangerous, that what they have planned can destroy the entire world. What makes you think two witches can stop an entire coven that's been around for ages?"

More silence.

I nudged my mom and felt her head loll to the side, landing on my shoulder. The soft sound of snores filled the air. Lifting her chin, I shook my head and settled her in to lie on the bench, then covered her with the spare blanket under my feet. I'd need to get Joe to help me carry Mom inside before she froze to death.

Tipping my head back, I rested it on the back of the bench and glared at the ceiling. At this rate, the world would end by the time I fished the truth out of my mother. I was running out of patience. The entire night reminded me of why the two of us didn't get along in the first place. We were too different; her very flighty and me constantly on edge. There was no way this partnership would work.

If I had any chance of surviving Sylvie Addison, I needed her out of the house. And fast.

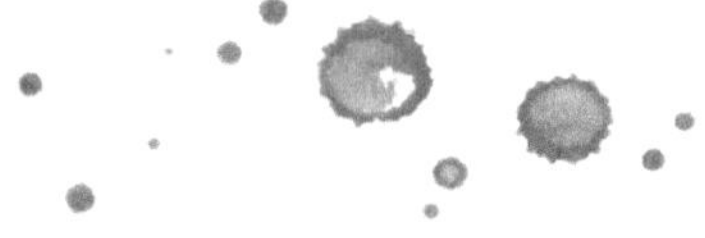

I awoke to the sound of banging around downstairs. My mind stirred out of sleep, fighting against my energized body. I vaguely recalled the dream I had— nightmare was more like it— and shook it off, swinging my legs around to see what all the commotion was about.

On my way out of the bedroom, I grabbed the closest thing I could think of to a weapon, a belt hanging off the door handle, then put it back. My best defense was my magic. If I could get it to work, that is.

It took a second for my eyes to adjust to the dim light, but when they did, I wanted to scream.

The raccoon had completely destroyed my kitchen.

Cupboards were left open, drawers pulled out, and there was a white powder sprinkled all over the floor. The rascal got into the sugar bag again. I stifled an angry growl, my eyes catching a set of paw prints on the trail of sugar. From where I stood, they led directly into the backyard.

"Gotcha!"

Snagging the broom, I wrapped my robe tightly over my body and bolted through the rear door. My feet padded softly against the mismatched cobblestone path leading to the greenhouse, and I was very aware of how cold my toes were. *Why the heck didn't I put on shoes?* No matter. I was going to show the furry sneak who the boss of this house was once and for all.

I could see the greenhouse loom before me, growing taller as I approached it. A light lit within and I paused. Something was wrong. Raccoons didn't use candles.

Step by shaky step, I got closer to the glass encasing of the greenhouse, ducking the entire way. Did I leave a candle on in there? I wasn't certain, but it'd been a while since I stepped foot in the place, so I doubted it. My heart raced and banged against my ribcage and my hands were slick with sweat. I pressed my nose against the glass and shimmied down until only my head was poking over the wood frame. Breath coming short, I peered inside.

Indoors, a dozen candles sat at different heights, illuminating the greenhouse in a golden glow. The plants I let go to waste crowded old pots like creepy carcasses, watching what went on.

"What in the..."

In the center of the greenhouse stood my mother. Her hair was untied, slightly swaying as she chanted words I didn't understand over and over. Beneath her, a circle of ash and soot was cast, five more candles marking the points of the pentagram.

I swallowed a gasp.

This had all the makings of dark magic; the same magic my mother so adamantly told me she wanted to put a stop to when she infiltrated the Sisters of the River. Was she lying? Did she switch sides?

My throat was suddenly bone dry.

I had been housing with a dark witch and I didn't even realize it. I was about to confront her when Sylvie raised her hand and a glint of silver caught my eye. My jaw hit the ground as she swung a ceremonial dagger in the air and brought it back down, nicking her left palm in the process. My mother held her hand over the circles and I gagged as blood poured from her wound.

All around her, a bright blue light exploded. I had to shield my eyes and duck further down to keep it from obliterating my vision. When the light dispersed, I began to pull myself up, but a clamor stopped me in my tracks.

On the side of the house, hanging by the drain-pipe, was Harry Houdini. His little legs kicked out as he attempted to crawl further up, only to slide down again. He was making so much noise, I knew he would get me caught. Not bothering to keep spying, I jumped up and ran into the house. When I got inside, I slammed the door shut behind me and pressed my back into the wood, sliding my butt to the floor.

Tears stung the back of my eyelids; I fought to keep them at bay.

My mother was a liar. Worse, she may be one of the Sisters and working against me to... Well, I didn't know what. Whatever it was, it couldn't be anything good. The entire scenario confirmed what I already knew in my gut: Sylvie Addison was not to be trusted. Not before and definitely not now.

Thank you, Harry, I thought before going back upstairs where I laid in bed with my eyes wide open until the sun broke.

CHAPTER 5

Harry Houdini

An absolute ruckus interrupted my slumber. My belly was full from the roll of salami I managed to snake away from the witch's kitchen while she wasn't home and I was hoping for a proper nap before the night began.

Unfortunately, the doors creaking open in my house of glass prevented it.

I opened one eye to look through the small opening between the two ceramic flower boxes hiding me from view. Long fabric the color of a rainbow whooshed along the ground, almost hitting me in the nose. I scooted backward, my hind legs wedged uncomfortably under my belly. From here, I could make out the face of the intruder easily.

I snapped my teeth at the older witch, but she couldn't hear me over the noise she was making. How frustrating. I really needed to remember there were two of them now. Just my luck, the fire-haired chaos makers were multiplying.

A smell I knew all too well permeated the air and I inched further into the shadows. In moments, my hideaway was lit up as the witch moved swiftly to summon the light she'd brought with her. She stepped sideway, knocking one of the waxy contraptions over, and cursed under her breath. If she wasn't careful, we'd both go up in flames.

Frustration made my stomach growl. How long had it been since dinner? Too long. I started for the hole I used to get in and out of the hideaway, but stopped.

Something shiny glistened in the light, demanding my attention. Paws padding the ground, I belly-crawled under the bench to get closer to the object. It was round and a brilliant gold, all the things I loved to covet. My arm stretched forward, reaching, reaching...

Snap!

The witch tossed the object into a box and shut the lid. Foolishness!

Hissing low breaths, I watched her pull another

object out of her pocket, this one much less interesting. It was a piece of paper with the likeness of a man on it; one I didn't recognize. It wasn't the one smelling of false blood who visited the young witch so often. This man appeared to be older, scrawnier, and less inviting.

I hated him immediately.

Sniffing the air, my feelings were confirmed. Even the smell of the piece of paper was foul. Spicy with a hint of pickle juice. Grotesque.

My stomach growled again, urging me to move along. As I did, the witch whispered words I couldn't hear and my eyes darted to the sliver of blue light forming in the air before her. The witch's eyes widened, and she stared into the light like it was a freshly baked cookie.

Hmm... cookie.

I really needed to get a move on.

The same smell from before drifted from the light and I scurried away before I lost my appetite. Only one thing could turn this night around. I needed to get into the young witch's lair of goods and get my hands on the white powder she hid from me. It was the only thing to make me forget that stench.

And the fact that her older twin was destroying my only sanctuary in this place.

Witches. Yuk.

The sun barely peeked through the clouds when I revved up the Beetle and gunned it out of the driveway. Dust in my rear-view, I stepped on the gas and drove as fast as I could, putting more distance between myself and the farmhouse. What I witnessed in the greenhouse last night had me on edge and I had no intention of seeing Mom this morning.

I was pretty sure she'd be sleeping until noon, anyway. A bottle of wine and a dose of dark magic tended to tire people out.

Flashes of Sylvie slicing her palm ran through my mind. I held the steering wheel in a death grip as I battled the incoming memories. "Why, Mom? Why do you always have to do these things?"

"What happened this time?"

The voice in the backseat scared me senseless, and it took all of my control not to steer the car off the cliffside road and into the sea below. My chest rose up and down as I heaved to catch my breath. I glanced in the mirror, scowling. "Good morning, Stella. Excellent way to start the day."

With an uninterested expression on her face, the ghost gazed at the sea, her overfilled lips puckered.

"Where were you last night?" I asked, breaking the eerie quiet.

The ghost's jaw tensed slightly. She rapped a gray finger on the window, the tapping sound that followed making her smile. Stella was almost entirely solid today; whatever she got up to the night before did wonders for her mood, it seemed. She rolled her tongue over her front teeth, sucking in a breath. "Here and there," replied the ghost, waving her hand vaguely. "There was too much excitement in the house for my liking."

We were back to non-answers then. I really thought that after I'd helped catch Stella's killer and ex-fiancé that she would open up more. But I was beginning to realize that this was simply who Stella Rutherford was; all riddles and no clues.

I pulled my gaze away from her and settled it on the winding road ahead.

"Ugh, I know," I said. "My mom found the liquor cabinet and Joe came by and—"

"Sylvie met the boyfriend?"

White-knuckles gripping the wheel, I avoided the fact that the ghost's eyebrows were hiked so high they were touching her hairline. "She did, and that wasn't even the worst part. I caught her working what looked like a dark magic spell in the greenhouse at night."

"No!" the ghost exclaimed.

"Yes!"

"No!"

I groaned. "We're not doing that. Anyway, I'm pretty sure that her and Mrs. Cevil are up to no good. Mom said the baker— who's a witch by the way, shocker!— is helping her stop the Sisters, but after what I witnessed, I think they might be working with the coven instead of against it."

Giving Stella a chance to wrap her mind around everything I word-vomited, I veered off the main road and took the exit to Cliff Row. The dashboard clock read six in the morning, way earlier than what I was used to. Unfortunately, today was not a day for sleeping in, not if I wanted to get to the bottom of what Sylvie and Mrs. Cevil were up to.

Slowing the car, I rolled down the window to get some fresh air and a bit of courage.

"What's your plan?" Stella asked from the backseat.

"Talk to Mrs. Cevil," I answered. "I have an order to pick up today, and I think I can catch her off guard. Get her to spill all their dirty little secrets before Mom has a chance of stopping her from speaking with me."

The street was already bustling with activity despite the early hour. I spotted Cilia on her way in for her shift at the hotel and waved as I drove by. The witch grinned widely, waving back before making a "call me" motion with her hand. I looked in the rearview. "Looks like I'll be out for drinks with Cilia again this weekend."

"Darling, if you are attempting to make me jealous, may I remind you I was the one who suggested you get a life?"

A vein popped in my forehead. "Whatever, we're here. Are you going to come in, or was this a taxi ride into town for you?"

"I suppose I could join you," Stella said, inspecting her perfect set of manicured nails.

Parking quickly, I rushed across the street and toward Bakes and Cakes. My fingers looped around the handle, quickly realizing my mistake. There was no way Mrs. Cevil would have the bakery open to the public yet. I was about to knock when a peculiar object caught my attention.

"What is taking so long?" Stella asked from behind me.

I pointed at the sliver of light shining through the door. "It's open."

"Wonderful work, detective."

"It shouldn't be open this early. I usually have to knock and wait a while until Mrs. Cevil comes out from the kitchen."

Crooking her long neck to peek inside, the ghost held up a slender finger and vanished momentarily. She reappeared a second later, scaring the bejesus out of me. "No one home."

"Impossible."

Pushing the door ajar, I slid into the bakery, my heart thumping in my chest. The overhead light flickered when I came in and goosebumps crawled over every inch of my body. *Danger, danger, danger!* my brain screamed as I made my way through the bubble gum interior.

The first thing that made me want to pee my pants were the overturned chairs in my way. Two were upside down and thrown across the bakery floor as though someone had knocked them over in a hurry. My thighs tensed in my jeans. "This feels wrong."

"You should see this."

I followed Stella's voice to the front counter where she stood with her finger pointing at the open register. A register that was completely emptied out.

"Oh, no…" I whispered at the same time as Stella said, "You should get the heck out of here."

Instead of listening to my familiar's wise words, I ventured further inside. My hands reached into my purse and I dug out my cellphone, pulling up the sheriff's number in case I needed to dial it urgently. On my free hand, lightning sparked wildly as my magic came out to play. If the robber was still here, I could zap their sorry behind and call the police. Finally, something I could do that was useful for a change.

Step by shaky step, I walked down the same corridor I often took toward the kitchen. Before reaching it, a door left ajar caught my attention, and I skidded to a fast stop in front of it.

"What is it?" Stella asked, appearing beside me.

My voice shook when I said, "The walk-in fridge is open."

Was Mrs. Cevil hiding out in there? Did she hear the intruder and lock herself in the fridge until they were gone? If she did, why was the door open? I did not like where this was going.

Palm flat on the metal, I pushed it open an inch at a time. "Mrs. Cevil? Is everything all right in there?"

No answer.

I tried again. "Reeba?"

Exchanging a look with Stella, I used my shoulder to wedge the fridge door fully open and stepped inside. My heart gave a jolt as my bones left my body. I wanted to turn around and run away, out of the fridge and out of the horrible scene I walked in on.

I couldn't move.

Stella Rutherford speed-talked instructions, but I couldn't hear her. All I could do was bite my quivering lip and blink away the tears that refused to stop falling.

A few feet away from me, Mrs. Cevil lay on the floor, motionless. Her hair, that was usually up in a bun, was undone and lay around her in gray ringlets. In her hand, a ladle was clutched so tight, her fingers had turned white. That wasn't the part that I couldn't take my eyes off.

What had my attention was the stainless steel cake tester sticking out of the center of her chest.

CHAPTER 7

"Amt te or sos taupe en ooh am in?"

Muffled words carried through the air, barely reaching my ears. My armpits were sweaty and there was a wet streak running down my back, soaking my sweater. I forced my wide, red eyes to turn away from the body bag and face the sheriff. "Sorry, what was that?"

"I asked if the door was open when you came in?" Sheriff Romero repeated.

"Which one?"

He looked at the walk-in fridge, then glanced over my shoulder at the front entrance. "Both."

"The front door was unlocked but closed," I

replied. "I only noticed the fridge door when I went to check on Mrs. Cevil after discovering the register."

"Which was emptied out?"

The sheriff noted every word out of my mouth on the notepad he often kept on hand. I was so used to this part, it was embarrassing. At this point, anyone who wanted to commit murder in our town should assume I'd be first on the scene. What was it about me and finding dead bodies? Maybe Stella was right— I was a magnet for trouble.

One of the deputies helped the coroner, a dusty old man who wore a suit to the crime scene, raised the stretcher, and they wheeled Mrs. Cevil's body out of the bakery. My stomach twisted into knots.

That poor woman.

"Miss Addison?"

I shook myself back to reality, my chest aching. "Yes, sorry. The register was empty. It looked like someone may have robbed the place."

Romero looked up from his notes, his eyes set in shadow from the brim of his large hat. I noticed he shaved off the mustache he usually sported; how strange to see so much of the man's face. I wondered if there were a special occasion for his new appearance, perhaps a date with a special someone? Then promptly scolded myself for thinking about the sheriff's love life while Mrs. Cevil was being loaded into an ambulance outside.

What was wrong with me?

"Do you know if Reeba usually kept a lot of cash on hand?" the sheriff asked.

First name, huh? Interesting. The question gave me pause because I hadn't given it much thought before. Once Stella and I saw the register, I assumed someone pocketed the cash and ran out. But how much money could a bakery possibly have at the end of the day?

I glanced at the register. "I can't be sure, though I doubt it was very much. Most businesses on the street tend to deposit their cash daily," I said. "I see them all the time in the bank when I drop off the money from the cafe."

Tipping his hat, Romero shoved the notepad into his back pocket. He walked the perimeter of the bakery, then down the corridor leading to the kitchen, disappearing from view. A few agonizing minutes passed before he reappeared holding an evidence bag. I strained my neck to see what was inside, bile rising in my throat when I realized it was the cake tester that killed Mrs. Cevil.

The sheriff briskly walked by me, stepped halfway out of the bakery, and held his arm out. When he pulled it back in, the evidence bag was gone and his sour expression was back.

He gestured for me to join him at one of the tables near the bay window.

"I have to ask, Miss Addison," Romero said after I sat across from him. "Is there anything you may have noticed that would make this... a matter of the witch variety?"

Excuse you? How did the sheriff know about Mrs. Cevil when I only just found out myself? The police weren't exactly in on the paranormal community, though Sheriff Romero was hired specifically because of his knowledge of my kind. Not that he was an expert in the matters of the things that go bump in the night, despite all his trying. In fact, after the last few cases I'd helped him solve, Romero enlisted me as his go-to for all crime involving the paranormal. I was kind of his resident informant, which was pretty sweet on days when I didn't walk into murder scenes out of the blue.

I quirked a brow and spread my fingers wide on the table. "You knew Mrs. Cevil was a witch?"

"Reeba and I had been friends for a long time," the sheriff answered.

The latte I had for breakfast came rushing up my throat and I had to bite down hard to stop it from making a second appearance. "I didn't realize. I'm so sorry for your loss."

"Thank you. Now, about my question..."

"Right. No," I said, "there's nothing here that appears to be driven by magic. To be honest, if my mother didn't tell me, I'd never have even known Mrs. Cevil was a witch."

The sheriff's pen stopped writing. "Your mother is back in town?"

Oops.

"Trust me, I was as surprised as you to see her. She won't be staying long," I said. Then added, "I hope."

"Ah, well, tell her I said hello."

Apparently, there was no need to pass on the message. A moment after the sheriff finished the sentence, the door swung open and none other than Sylvie Addison greeted us with her presence. Her hair was braided loosely at the nape of her neck and I was relieved to see she swapped the scarf skirt for form-fitting jeans and cowboy boots. For someone who drank half her weight in wine last night, my mother looked fantastic.

She spread her arms wide and went to hug the sheriff, stopping short of the uncomfortable exchange to shake his hand instead. "Hank! It is a pleasure to see you again," Mom said warmly. "Though I do wish it was under better circumstances."

Seriously? Hank? How did this woman know everyone I saw on a daily basis by first name?

Scanning the bakery with a quick turn, my mother looped around and pulled up a chair beside me. With her legs crossed and a stern look plastered on her face, she resembled an attorney coming to my rescue. As Romero flipped to a new page in his notebook, Mom nudged my side, making a motion with her fingers to indicate I should zip it.

I wasn't sure why she was acting so strange. Romero was on our side; he was one of the good guys.

Besides, it wasn't like I had anything to hide.

Paying her dramatic actions no mind, I focused on the elephant in the room. Turning halfway so I could face her head-on, I fixed Mom with a serious glare of my own and asked, "How did you know where to find me?"

"Your assistant at the cafe said you'd be here. Have you seen her new hair, by the way? The purple is fabulous."

The illusion spell Rory was working on must have been a hit. It was a shame I missed it. With everything that went on this morning, I never even had a chance to stop by Bean Me Up. I had to call Rory to come in, even though she wasn't scheduled to stop by until later in the afternoon. Lucky it was Sunday, or I'd have to close the cafe down for the day and I couldn't afford to take any more days off. Magic or not, bills didn't pay themselves. Not even in Orchard Hollow.

"I need to make a quick call and then I have a few more questions," the sheriff said.

As he pulled his chair out and walked out of our earshot, my mother tugged my sleeve. "Don't say a word about the Sisters or what Reeba and I were working on."

I frowned. The last thing I needed was a reminder of the stupid coven my mother may or may not have joined for real.

"Why not?" I asked. "Romero knows about para-normals. We don't have to hide things from him, if that's what you're afraid of."

"Hank knows? You don't say..."

I nodded slowly, ripping my arm out of her grip. "He does, so, if you don't mind, I'd rather not start lying to the police unless I can help it."

"Piper!" Mom exclaimed. "Please tell me I didn't raise you to be this naive. If the Sisters can get to Reeba, there's no telling what else they can do. Hank doesn't have magic. He can't protect himself the way we can. If you speak a word of this to him, you will be putting him in danger. Is that what you want?"

I gulped. Shame colored my cheeks red, and I swallowed the large lump forming at the base of my throat. I hadn't even considered that Mrs. Cevil's death may have something to do with the Sisters of the River. Sure, she and Mom were being sketchy, but for it to be bad enough to get killed over? Why didn't I think of that?

Stomach settling, I checked for the sheriff, who continued to be busy with the phone call. "You think they did this?" I whispered.

"Honey, which part of everyone is in danger was unclear? You need to steer Hank clear of it, and you need to do it now. Before he gets in over his head."

My chin pressed into my collarbone and I sucked in a sharp breath. "Look around, Mom. There's no sign of magic anywhere. I already checked."

"Don't be foolish. They wouldn't leave a trace behind."

Sighing, I rested my forehead on the table, banging it once to make the entire day disappear. It didn't work. When I came back up, I was still in the bakery with my mother's expectant eyes burrowing deep into my soul. "Okay, what's your plan?"

"Tell the sheriff there's nothing magical about this crime," she said. "And we pick up where Reeba and I left off."

My head spun three sixty at her suggestion. It wasn't that she wanted me to lie to the sheriff, not at all. As far as I was concerned, there really wasn't anything magical about the way Mrs. Cevil died. The register was emptied out, and she was killed, quite awfully, with a weapon of convenience. My opinion didn't change simply because my mother disagreed with it. What had me speechless was that Mom wanted me to keep on with whatever she and the baker were up to before she was killed.

There were three ways this could go down.

First, Mrs. Cevil died from the unfortunate circumstance of going up against whoever robbed her bakery. The second, was that I was right and my mom was part of the Sisters of the River, and this entire thing was a ruse to get me on their side. The last option, and the scariest, was Mom didn't lie about their plan and it got one of them killed. This part was the one that had me shaking in my boots. As Mom said, if the Sisters could get to Mrs. Cevil, a witch who'd been practicing longer than either of us, what's stopping them from going after us?

I let my eyes drift to the sheriff.

Perhaps keeping him in the dark was the best play after all. At least until I knew what truly happened here and how my mother was involved. I didn't trust her as far as I could throw her, but at this point, it was either work with her or stumble in the dark on my own. Neither option had me jumping for joy.

In my periphery, I saw Romero hang up the phone and walk toward us, his notebook already in his hands.

Nodding once at my mother, I waited until he sat down and was about to start Operation Lying Witch Face when my phone rang in my purse. I pulled it out, apologizing to the sheriff to answer. "Joe, hi. I was going to call you soon."

"Morning. I have some bad news."

What now? Stars exploded behind my eyes as I considered the lineup of bad that could follow the horrible morning I was already having. My heart beat fast and my thighs squeezed together so tight they hurt. I didn't think I could handle any more bad news.

"I have to leave for a week," Joe said.

My body slightly relaxed. That wasn't as terrible as I was expecting. Granted, I was likely expecting another murder, considering where I was at the moment. I loosened my grip on the phone and asked, "Is everything all right?"

"It will be," Joe answered. "A bit of a situation in King City with an old client. I should only be gone for a week, but I wanted to let you know so you're not worried."

"When do you leave?"

Joe cleared his throat. "I'm on my way there now. Sorry to spring this on you. It was urgent."

"Oh?"

"I'll explain it all when I get back," he said, sensing the worry in my voice. "How's your morning?"

Avoiding my mom and the sheriff, I settled my growing nerves and forced out a smile. "I might have to fill you in later as well. If you can sneak away for a phone call this evening, let's catch up then."

"Sounds good," Joe said. A horn honked on the other line, and he cursed. "Sorry, Piper. I have to let you go. Talk tonight."

Hanging up, I kept my gaze on the tabletop and away from the sheriff. A loose hangnail on my thumb begged for my attention and I tugged at it as I rolled the options around in my head. While I wasn't convinced the Sisters of the River had anything to do with what happened to Mrs. Cevil, I'd be foolish not to consider it. I side-glanced at my mother. It looked that I was stuck with her for a while longer.

Okay, I told myself. *New plan. Find out who killed Mrs. Cevil, get the truth out of Mom, and redirect the sheriff's attention so I can get it all done before someone else dies. Easy peasy.*

CHAPTER 8

I should have known that getting Sylvie Addison involved would only lead to illegal activity. Or, as my mother liked to call it, the gray areas of the law. As we stood outside of Bakes and Cakes and stared at the criss-crossing yellow tape across the door, butterflies fluttered in my stomach. The street was as dark as a cave, with only a few streetlamps to illuminate the two creepers hanging around well after midnight.

I sighed and looked at Mom standing beside me. Dressed in all black, she looked like a cat burglar from an old movie and not the loud-dressing woman I grew up with. Even her makeup was toned down. Gone was the blue glitter eye shadow and bright-painted nails. In their place was a streak of black on both her eyes and a nude lipstick that did nothing for her complexion.

Mom was taking this way too seriously.

"Ready?" asked Sylvie.

I narrowed my eyes at the tape, shrugging. "Is this really the best idea? What if we get caught?"

"Honey, what did I always tell you? Think positive to stay positive," my mother said as though her words of wisdom helped us in our current situation.

"I don't think that applies to breaking and entering," I retorted.

Instead of answering, Sylvie pulled aside the tape, looked around, and turned the bakery door handle. Before I could object, she slipped inside and out of view. My heart raced as I followed her in. *Here we go.*

Upon leaving the bakery earlier today, the idea of sneaking in after everyone left seemed to be a great one. In fact, I was almost proud of my mother for suggesting it. Now that I stood here in the dark with only my quivering breath for company, I had quite the opposite reaction.

This was without a doubt the dumbest thing I'd ever done.

"Move it or lose it, honey," Mom called from further inside.

A growl got trapped in my throat and for a moment I considered turning on my heels and storming out, leaving her by herself. An image of Sylvie behind bars and the sheriff reading her her rights ran through my head. I grimaced. It wasn't Mom's fault I agreed to go through with her half-cocked plan.

Shaking off the residual nerves rattling in my brain, I squared my shoulders and followed her into the darkness. The quicker we could get done searching the place, the quicker I could get back home and put the night behind me. No matter what Mom said, I was certain we would find no evidence of magic in the bakery. If partaking in highly questionable activities got Sylvie off my back about the Sisters of the River, I was willing to go along with it. Especially since I still didn't know if I could trust Mom to tell the truth about the coven.

Perhaps while I was here, I could look for evidence to help me clear her name. Unless she lied about working with Mrs. Cevil.

Anything was possible.

A dull yellow glow sparked a few feet ahead and suddenly Mom's face appeared, illuminated by a candle. I cocked my head to the side. "Where did you get that?"

"Always come prepared," she replied, pointing to a small backpack strapped to her shoulders. "You never know what you might need."

I rolled my eyes. Leave it to my mother to be prepared for what we were doing here. I felt instantly foolish for not thinking ahead and showing up with nothing but my cellphone's flashlight in tow. In my defense, Sylvie was much more adept in the art of shifty business, so one couldn't possibly blame me for not knowing what to pack to break into a crime scene. Not like we were going on a cruise over here.

Motioning to the rear of the bakery, my mother slithered down the corridor and disappeared from view. I took that as my cue to search the front area.

Hands shaking, I clicked on the light on my phone and got down to business. I had no clue what to look for or where to start, but the front counter seemed as good a place as any. Keeping my eyes on the bay window and the street beyond, I snuck behind the counter and started to search.

There was nothing out of the ordinary that I could spot. A stack of papers near the register revealed a list of names with corresponding baked goods beside them. I saw my own name on the list and realized this must have been Mrs. Cevil's bulk order forms. Putting the papers away, I moved down the counter. By the time I got to the end, all I had to show for my effort were more order forms and a few business cards clients had left behind. I read them quickly, a few sparking some recognition. My fingers tapped the edges of Isabella Beaumont's card. The owner of the Rose Hollow Hotel and Cilia's boss, who also happened to be a vampire. I vividly remembered Joe urging me to stay away from her, and my skin cooled at the thought.

What was Mrs. Cevil doing with a vampire's business card?

I put the pile down, pocketing Isabella's card, and moved on. The remainder of the bakery's front had no hidden clues. I was about to check how Mom was faring and if she had better luck when my magic exploded on my fingertips. A pulsing ache pounded at the space between my ears as the lightning I accidentally summoned intensified. I shook my hands, but the magic remained, crawling up my arms.

"What is happening now?"

Attempting to rein the magic in did nothing, and it only got brighter and stronger. The pain I felt before intensified and I buckled back, my shoulders hitting the solid wall behind me. Confusion laced through me. *Was I allergic to my own brand of magic now?* That seemed unlikely.

To my right, the air rippled. I swung my head over to see it rip apart like someone was opening a zipper. *Not this again,* I thought, recalling the last time this happened. It had been a while since I'd seen a rift and when they didn't return, I chalked it up to the malfunctioning of my magic. Maybe it was too hasty to do that since the tear was clearly back and bigger than before.

The one in front of me was almost the size of a door, and it was growing by the second. Something zoomed across inside the rift and I stifled a scream. It was so dark that it was impossible to make anything out, but I was sure I saw someone run by. My eyes widened in terror.

A hard object hit my side and knocked me over. Losing balance, I tumbled to the ground, breaking my fall with my lightning-covered hands. Near me, a ball of hardened dough rolled away, and I winced, realizing that was what hit me.

"Close it down! Now!" my mother screamed, her arm extended from the dough throw.

I shook my head. "I don't know how!"

Looping around behind me, she grabbed my arms and used me as a marionette. Sylvie's voice rose in my ears as she spewed words in a language I didn't understand. When she thrust my arms forward, lightning exploded from them, shooting into the dark rift growing in front of us. It vibrated and closed down in a flash as though nothing was there to begin with.

Sweat dripped down my forehead in buckets. I sagged against my mother, my eyes never leaving the empty space where the rip was seconds ago. "What was that?" I asked between breaths.

"Nothing good," Sylvie replied. "Was it the first time you'd seen one?"

"No. There were a few before but they haven't been back. Are you saying you know what they are?"

Sylvie bit her lip and looked at the ground. The candle she sat on the floor flickered between us, adding a surreal atmosphere to an already strange night. My mother picked it up carefully and ran her finger over the flame as she said, "If the doorways are opening, they must be getting close."

"What doorways?"

Mom sighed, her entire body releasing the breath she was holding. "To summon Hades, the Sisters must open the door to the Underworld," she explained. "What you saw was a small tear between the realms. If the coven were to succeed, there's no telling how big of a doorway they might open. Or what might come through."

"Hold on," I said. "You're telling me the rips are actual openings into the Underworld? It exists somewhere out there?"

Running her finger through the flame again, Mom said, "Here, there. Everywhere. The Underworld is not a place you can find on a map, honey."

My jaw locked, teeth gnashing together.

"How can you act so nonchalant about this? And why am I the one seeing these stupid doorways?"

"I have been dealing with the Sisters for years, talking about their evil ways is nothing new," Mom reminded me. "The last time I was with them in Ridgewood, the witches nearly burned down a hospital trying to open one of those things. But we should get a move on, don't you think? Or would you rather discuss the coven at a murder scene?"

I would rather not be in a position where I had to discuss anything with my mother at all, especially not a coven that was apparently trying to open the gateway to Hell. What a complete disaster. As much as I wanted to grill Sylvie right there and then, she was right. Hanging around in the dark of the bakery was not the best plan. For all I knew, the sheriff would come around again and if he were to find us here, all the trust I had worked hard to build between us would go out the window. Worse, I would never be able to steer him away from the Sisters of the River as Mom wanted me to do if we're caught snooping around looking for magic.

Frowning, I stood up and dusted off my jeans. "You can tell me more on the way home," I told Mom. "The front was clear. Did you find anything in the back?"

A Cheshire grin spread across Sylvie's face. With

the candle right under her face and the way her eyes were painted, she resembled a clown from a horror movie. I stifled a laugh, giving her a chance to speak.

Reaching into her back pocket, Mom pulled out a folded piece of paper, unfolded it and shoved it in my face. "Do you know someone by the name of Brandy Doll?" she asked.

"Not that I can think of," I replied. "Why?"

She tapped the paper, still smiling. "Because according to this, she had a bakery on the other end of Cliff Row and she wasn't too happy with Reeba stealing all her customers."

"Okay," I said, squinting to make out what the handwritten note said. "A rival business is nothing new in this town. I don't see how their small spat is important to the case."

The smile dropped from my mother's face. She shook the paper in front of my face and said, "This was hidden behind the cake fridge. It's a letter from Brandy telling Reeba to close her bakery or she'll be sorry."

I snatched the paper from her hands and read over it quickly, confirming everything Mom said. The writing was neat and tidy, indicating that Brandy took time to put her words on paper. She even used her bakery's branded stationery to write the note on. The words Muffin Stop were stamped in gold lettering across the top with a picture of a muffin wearing sunglasses below it. A cute touch.

"You think Brandy Doll killed Mrs. Cevil over a shop dispute?"

Mom arched one eyebrow, giving me a look that summarized exactly what I was thinking. Mrs. Cevil was dead and a competing business was a damn good lead. Considering what I'd seen lately, people have certainly killed for less.

CHAPTER 9

The spoon clinked against the steaming mug in my hand while my mom busied herself in the kitchen, attempting to make an omelette that more closely resembled scrambled eggs. Sitting beside me at the kitchen table, Stella watched intently as I added a second dash of brown sugar into my Gingerbread Latte and stirred. Clink. Clink. Clink.

"Did the coffee cup wrong our family somehow?" Stella asked.

I continued to stir, hoping the spinning coffee would somehow stop my mind from racing. On the way home from our less than honest investigation session, Mom wouldn't stop talking my ear off. She ran scenario after scenario, all of which ended in one conclusion— that Brandy Doll was somehow working for the coven. My mother was so intent on Mrs. Cevil's death being the result of the Sisters, she refused to entertain other ideas.

For me, what happened to the baker wasn't so cut and dry.

While I wasn't a detective, or had any real knowledge of police procedures, there was one thing I was fairly certain of and the thought wouldn't leave me alone. Mrs. Cevil was stabbed in the heart with a cake tester. A horrific way to go that said more about the killer than Mom was willing to think about. If the coven was responsible for the crime, they certainly wouldn't resort to brute force. From what my mother told me, which wasn't much, the Sisters of the River may be the oldest living coven around. That fact alone would make them incredibly powerful.

Wouldn't they use magic to do their bidding instead? Surely we were barking up the wrong tree here.

The more I thought about the scene I'd walked in on, the more I realized the killer had to be someone Mrs. Cevil knew well. A friend. Or even a family member. To stab someone in the heart was a passionate choice for a murder and one that I highly doubted any self-respecting witch would succumb to.

Not that I would ever consider hurting anyone, but even *I* would use magic over anything else if it came down to it.

My brain hurt. Nothing about this case was adding up.

Hands clapped in my face, startling me enough that I jumped in my seat. The spoon I held bounced off the edge of the cup and tumbled to the floor. I bent down to catch it, my forehead slamming the side of the kitchen table. "Ouch!" I yelped, rubbing the already growing bump. *That's going to leave a mark.* My eyes trickled up to my familiar, whose transparent hands were still clasped together. "Was that necessary?"

"You're one step away from zombie town," she said with a grimace. "It was either that or I get Sylvie over there to slap you with the pan."

My attention flitted to my mother, who stood by the stove, oblivious to the two of us. In her ears, headphones blared music from the seventies I didn't know the lyrics to. Sylvie's body swayed from side to side as she attempted to flip her eggs in the air, failing miserably. A piece fell off and got trapped in her hair without her noticing. I was instantly reminded of where I got my clumsiness from.

"Two peas in a pod," my ghost familiar said.

I waved a hand through her arm and she winced.

"Never say that again," I warned. "Want to get out of here?"

"Where to?" Stella asked.

Downing my latte in two big gulps, I set the cup on the table, careful not to make a sound. My gaze stayed locked on my mother as I slowly slid out of the chair and motioned for Stella to follow me outside. We marched in unison, two silent birds hopping down a path. Well, one hopping bird and one floating ghost, but the sentiment stayed true; by the time we reached the door and slipped outside, Mom was none the wiser.

I zipped up my jacket and fought against the bite of the cold air to get to the car. Behind me, Stella vanished, reappearing in the backseat as usual. When I got in, she said, "Not that I'm complaining, but why are we ditching dear old Mom?"

Turning the ignition on, I rolled the Beetle out of the driveway at a pace slower than a snail's. "I want to check out a hunch and I don't want her in the way."

"Ah, the old bait and switch," Stella said, a wicked smile on her face. "What are we checking out?"

The house grew smaller in the distance, its cozy shape disappearing from my rear-view. "We're going to check out the other bakery in town," I told the ghost. "With Mrs. Cevil gone, I need a new supplier."

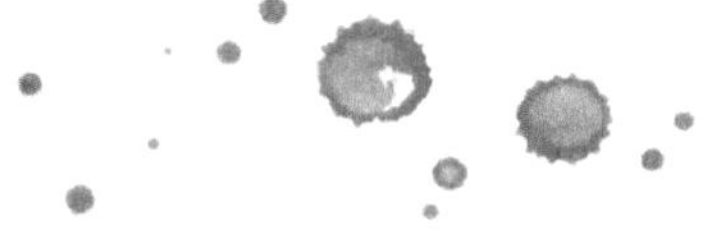

The Muffin Stop was a quaint, quiet place with an all-glass exterior and only a few tables set up in front of a small display counter. When I walked in, the first thing I noticed was how different the bakery was from Bakes and Cakes. Where Mrs. Cevil's shop had all the charm of a Parisian cafe, this place was modern and minimal, with no flourishes at all. White walls surrounded me and the only color in the entire space seemed to be reserved for the bright green menu on the wall behind the display case. Even the floors were a white tile with black grout, making me feel like I should have taken my shoes off when I entered.

"I absolutely love it here," Stella announced.

Of course, she did. Stella Rutherford enjoyed everything that smelled like money and the bakery reeked of high-end finishes.

I cast a quick glance at the bizarre, colorless abstract art on one wall and made my way to the counter. My head ticked to the side; even the baked goods looked like they were straight out of a futuristic movie set. Dark chocolate pyramids and perfect white truffle spheres sat on clear glass plates with only a drizzle of a sauce as their festive garnish. While I was certain each one would be delectable, I yearned for Mrs. Cevil's oversized muffins dripping with icing. For a place named after one of my favorite treats, Brandy's bakery did not have one muffin in stock.

"Hi, there," a high-pitched voice rang out from behind the counter. "What can I get you today?"

Swallowing the fear that I may actually have to eat one of the weird cakes, I looked up from the pastries and faced the woman before me. The server, who, judging from her name tag, was none other than Brandy herself, was not who I expected. A part of me was hoping to see another sweet, older woman with flour in her hair and a flowery apron tied around her waist. As it turned out, it wasn't only the bakery that was different.

Brandy's recently dyed blonde hair was tied back in an intricate braid that draped over her uncovered shoulder, following the curve of her low-cut top. She wore high-waisted leather pants which hugged every curve of her hips and had so much makeup on she looked more fit for a night out than running a bakery. I smiled awkwardly, rubbing my sweaty hands over my frizzy hair.

"You should take some pointers for date outfits while we're here," Stella whispered in my ear.

I waved a palm under the counter, shooing off the frustrating ghost, then looked up at Brandy. "Hello," I said, putting my game face on. "Do you, by any chance, take wholesale orders?"

"I certainly do!" the woman exclaimed. She returned my smile, but there was a slight tug on the edges of her lips, making it seem as though she was tired of being the face of the bakery. I wondered if putting on appearances was standard procedure for her. Before I could spiral down the guessing game, Brandy asked, "Would this be a standing order?"

I nodded in agreement. "It would be, yes. I have a cafe nearby and am looking for a new place to get my baked goods."

"Oh, how wonderful! Not the adorable space cafe, is it?"

Another nod. "That's me," I said.

"Oh, you were serious about the order," Stella mused over my shoulder. "I thought it was a cover to get information."

I battled between responding and pretending not to hear her to avoid looking especially unhinged. Behind the counter, Brandy lowered one brow and looked at me through hooded eyes, her expression expectant. If I didn't say something soon, it would raise too many red flags. My mind raced to remember what Brandy said before my familiar's rude interruption, but it was impossible to do with her breathing down my neck. I angled my body sideways, blocking out Stella's bored face. "It's not wildly busy," I finally uttered, "but it would be a regular order."

"That sounds wonderful," Brandy said. She pointed to the lineup of space treats. "Anything in particular you were interested in?"

I gulped. My chance had come. "I actually had a supplier before," I told the baker. "There was an unfortunate incident and now I am in the market for a new place."

Waiting for her to reply, I studied Brandy's face for some sign of guilt, but she barely blinked. Her lips puckered as understanding dawned on her and she gasped, her hand pressing to her chest.

"Oh, my," she breathed out. "You don't mean what happened to poor Reeba, do you?"

Slowly, I nodded.

"What an utter shame. And absolute tragedy, if you ask me," Brandy continued. "I tell you, this town used to be the safest place to live and look at us now. Death after death after death." She glanced out the window, her shoulders drooping. "It's a surprise we have people come visit."

As much as I wanted to, I couldn't argue with her logic. I'd seen my fair share of the dark underbelly of Orchard Hollow to wonder the same thing myself. With Brandy's attention on the street, I turned to

Stella, who shrugged in agreement. If only Brandy knew about the paranormals in our town...

My gaze traveled around the bakery again and over Brandy's attire to confirm what I already knew. No sign of magic and no family talisman; Brandy Doll was not a paranormal.

"Anyhoo," Brandy said with an exhale. "Were you close with Reeba?"

I bristled, wondering how much I should share. While I didn't think this woman had anything to do with Mrs. Cevil's murder— her demeanor didn't scream killer to me— it didn't mean I could trust her. I tucked a hair behind my ear and relaxed my anxious posture. "Not very," I replied. "She knew my mother, and I saw her a few times a week to pick up my order. Were you friends?"

Even though I already knew the answer, I gave Brandy the chance to respond.

"We were friendly enough."

The little liar. I tried my hardest to ignore the string of choice words that burst from Stella's mouth, concentrating on the baker. "Oh," I said, feigning surprise. "I was under the impression you two were competing businesses."

"Who told you that?"

I gestured to the street beyond the bakery. "You know how things are here."

"Unfortunately, I do," said Brandy. She shook her head, sighing. "I suppose it's no secret we were in competition. You can't blame us really, it's a small street. Only so many customers to go around. But I never wished her any harm."

Another lie. I was beginning to think I may have been wrong about the woman. Working my jaw, I formulated my response then said, "Do you know anyone who might have wanted to hurt Mrs. Cevil? It's such a shock. I'm trying to understand who would do that to such a sweet woman."

"Ha!" Brandy hollered, making me jump in shock. "Not to speak ill of the dead, but if you think Reeba was sweet, you've got your hair tied too tightly. That woman was a shark. She'd run you over to get her way and you can mark my word on it."

"Ding! Ding! Ding! We have ourselves a motive!" Stella yelled from behind me.

I focused on the alive woman in front of me instead of my very loud familiar. "I take it Mrs. Cevil got in your way?" I asked, adding, "on a business level."

"That's one way of putting it. Would you believe it if I told you Reeba tried to put me out of business?" Brandy said. "The nerve of her. Just because her bakery was drowning didn't mean she had to take me down with her. I mean, sure, we were the only two on the street, but I think you can agree that we did not have the same clientele."

The baker motioned to the display again for emphasis, her eyes rolling. "Didn't stop her from trying to out-do me every chance she got. Foolishness, if you ask me."

"What did you mean about Bakes and Cakes drowning?" I asked quickly.

"The place was barely hanging on. Not to toot my own horn, but since I opened my doors, a lot of Reeba's customers started coming here." Her eyes cast downward for a brief moment. "Although I did feel terrible, she had to take out a second mortgage on her house to stay afloat."

"And yet you threatened her anyway," I blurted out before I could stop myself.

"Wild move," Stella whispered.

In front of me, Brandy's expression soured, her entire face twisting in on itself. She looked me up and down, asking, "Reeba told you about the letter?"

"She spoke to my mom about it," I lied.

"It wasn't what you think," Brandy said, her voice barely a hush. "Reeba got aggressive, started coming after my customers. It wasn't a great look. Competition or not, I worried about her. A little over a month ago, I went to see her. That was when I found out about her money issues and how bad it had gotten. She told me she got a hefty loan to keep the bakery afloat and was having trouble paying it back."

I leaned into the counter, putting my entire weight on it. "I had no idea Bakes and Cakes was in that much trouble."

"Not the bakery," Brandy corrected. "Reeba was in trouble. The man she borrowed the money from, Tom Sorrelis, isn't a great guy. He's known to some of us on the street as being a financial piranha. A loan shark with zero conscience and even fewer morals."

My brow creased.

"You know, someone who'll eat you alive for the right price," Brandy said. "Anyhoo, that's who Reeba got the money from when the bank refused to work with her. I tried to talk her out of it, sent her the letter to try to convince to close shop before it got worse, but she wouldn't budge."

"How come?"

Brandy shrugged. "Once Reeba got an idea in her head, there was no stopping her. She was a captain that would go down with their ship, if you get my drift."

Butterflies fluttered in my belly and the hairs on the back of my neck stood tall. It seemed Mrs. Cevil went down with her ship after all. Money missing from the register, the bakery being in trouble, and her owing some scumbag a ton of cash? Did the man Mrs.

Cevil borrow from come to collect? It could explain the nature of the crime. If they got into an unexpected argument, someone labeled a financial piranha might take it upon himself to escalate things. Could the argument have turned to a physical altercation and Mrs. Cevil got hurt in the process?

It was a good theory.

"It's awful what happened to her," Brandy said. "I thought that we could become fast friends if she only got out of her own way."

It appeared Mrs. Cevil got into someone else's way instead. Fingers spread wide on the counter, I exhaled slowly, saying, "Do you think Tom could have hurt her over the money?"

"I can't say," she answered. "Anyhoo, about the order? I'm sure I've talked your ear off long enough."

I told the baker I'd take a sample order of several items to test out and get back to her with an answer, then took my box of weird cakes and walked out the door, Stella trailing close behind me. On the way home, the ghost sat quietly in the backseat, giving me some time to collect my thoughts. Brandy didn't strike me as someone who was angry enough to kill Mrs. Cevil and her explanation about the letter sounded convincing. That, combined with the lack of magic in the bakery, was enough to take her off the list; for me and for Mom. My mother was not going to be happy when I told her I went to see the baker without her, but it was the best play. Sylvie tended to go in all guns blazing and I was certain if I followed her lead, I wouldn't have the juicy piece of information I now had.

In my head, I crossed Brandy Doll's name off of an imaginary list and added another— Tom Sorrelis.

In the rear-view, Stella gave me a quick nod of approval, coming to the same conclusion as me. We had to find out all we could about the piranha. If he was responsible for Mrs. Cevil's death, who knew what else he could do? Brandy made it sound like more than one business "borrowed" money from the loan shark and if Sorrelis would kill an old woman over cash, everyone else who dealt with him could be in danger.

CHAPTER 10

"I can't believe you are sneaking around like a teenager! You should have waited for me," my mother said, fuming. She set down a ladle on the counter, the red pasta sauce on it leaving a stain I knew I'd never get out. "That woman could have been dangerous. I know you're starting to develop new powers, but your magic is no match for that of a Sister."

I groaned in exasperation. "For the tenth time, Brandy Doll is not a witch."

"Simply because you didn't see a talisman doesn't mean she isn't. She could have it hidden or she might not be the one in her family to have one," Mom rebutted. "You should know better, Piper."

"I do know better," I said. "It wasn't only that I didn't see one, I didn't feel it anywhere near her."

Head tilting sideways, Mom inspected me with intrigue, a note of confusion swimming behind her eyes. Right, I hadn't told her about this part of my strange magic yet. I crossed my arms, gritting my teeth as she picked up the dirty ladle only to set it down on another part of the counter. Behind her, the pasta sauce overflowed, and she turned off the stove without breaking eye contact with me.

Note to self, Mom is as intimidating as she was when I was a kid. So much so that my skin grew clammy. I wrapped the wool shawl I wore around my shoulders and said, "When I'm around a paranormal's talisman, it's like it calls to me. I can feel its magic. Sometimes even see it."

"Hmm. Interesting," Mom mused.

"Not really. The interesting part is that I was able to use the magic of another witch's talisman before."

The revelation earned me a double eyebrow raise and a gaping mouth. My mother tossed the ladle into the saucepan, causing it to splash all over the back counter. Forgetting all about our lunch, she pulled out a chair and sat opposite me at the table. "Why didn't you tell me this sooner?"

"It was a while ago and I hadn't exactly tested it since," I replied.

Sylvie scrunched her nose, her eyes narrowing. "What about Mom's brooch? Have you noticed a change in you when you're near it?"

"About that..."

I was about to break the news that our family talisman was shattered to pieces by a psychotic killer on one of my extracurricular escapades of playing detective when my phone rang. Holding up a finger, I clicked to answer it, my anticipation building. Usually when the sheriff's number flashed on my screen, I had quite a different reaction; one that was more akin to dread than excitement. Not this time. Earlier today I had asked Romero for help to track down Tom Sorrelis and I was really hoping for some good news.

I brought the phone to my ear, avoiding Mom's heated stare when I said, "Hello, Sheriff."

"Miss Addison," the sheriff said gruffly on the other end. "Have I caught you at a good time?"

"Of course. Were you able to get that information for me?"

There was a grumble followed by a long, heavy sigh on the line. I waited patiently while the sheriff worked out his frustration with me. I knew I was asking for a lot, more than he was likely allowed to do, but when Romero asked for my help with paranormal cases in Orchard Hollow, I made it clear that it was a two-way street. Now it was time to collect. The problem was that I couldn't tell him why I needed to know Tom's location and I especially couldn't divulge it now with my mother staring daggers at me from across the table.

A few more grumbles broke the silence before the sheriff finally spoke. "I was able to get a credit card purchase tracked for a Tom Sorrelis," he said. "Now, before I tell you what I have, please remind me again why this is so important."

"I'm following a lead," I said truthfully. "It's nothing yet, but I promise you shouldn't be concerned over it. And I'll be perfectly safe. I need to have a chat with Tom for a friend."

"Right. I must say, Miss Addison, I don't quite buy that," the sheriff remarked. "We have different definitions of perfectly safe, I'm afraid."

I winced, recalling all the times I assumed no harm would come out of certain situations to have the exact opposite happen. I rubbed my temples, fighting the tension headache forming behind my eyes. "It's truly nothing to worry about. I appreciate any help you can provide."

"A deal is a deal," Romero said gingerly. "The last time Tom Sorrelis used his card was right here in town. At the Rose Hollow Hotel."

You have got to be kidding me. This entire time, he'd been under my nose— or across the street— and

I didn't even know it. Not that I would, since I had no idea the man existed up until recently. Yet it felt like a wasted favor getting the sheriff involved for something so trivial. Granted, my online sleuthing didn't garnish any results, and I wasn't about to ask Joe to use his stellar social stalking skills for this. From the sound of our very brief conversation last night, whatever he was doing in the city had him exhausted, and I didn't want to be the one to add more to his plate. Plus, if Joe knew I was wrapped up in yet another murder investigation, he'd worry unnecessarily.

No, I had to do this on my own.

My attention caught on my mother across from me. *Ugh.* Not entirely on my own, I supposed. I looked down at a broken nail to tear myself away from Mom's death stare and asked, "Is he staying at the hotel?"

"That I couldn't tell you," the sheriff answered. "All I know is his card was last used there. You'll have to find out some other way what the purpose of the charge was."

A grin tugged at the corners of my lips. Lucky for me, I knew exactly how to go about doing just that. I thanked the sheriff for the information, promising one more time to stay out of trouble, then hung up the phone. As I pocketed it, my mother watched my every move, waiting for me to fill her in. There was no getting out of it this time— the woman was a dog with a bone now.

"Well?" she asked, her patience thinning out.

I rolled my eyes. "Get your coat on," I told her and rose to stand. "Let's go see a witch about a room."

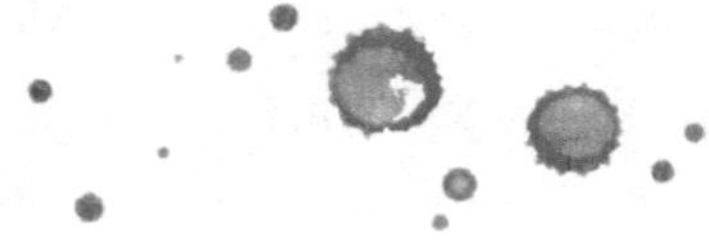

The Rose Hollow Hotel was exactly as I remembered it. A colonial style building that sat on a hefty portion of Cliff Row, directly opposite Bean Me Up. Each time I visited, I couldn't help but turn around to look at my cafe. It was an odd feeling to own a business considering that only a few years ago my life had zero direction.

My chest swelled with pride as I swung the hotel's wide doors open and stepped inside, my mother hurrying in behind me. Under my feet, the ornate carpet made tiny squeaking sounds as I walked, a loud noise in an otherwise quiet place. I marched past the two antique sofas making up the front seating area, nodding a polite hello at the group of tourists sitting there.

The main lobby split off in two directions, one leading to a bronze framed elevator which took guests up to their rooms and the other was a hallway I was yet to explore. I vividly recalled my last time sneaking around the hotel to search for evidence of a past crime committed here, and my stomach churned. At least today I had a friend working the front desk, and I didn't have to feel like Harry Houdini looking for snacks.

Making a beeline for reception, I checked left and right for Cilia, but she wasn't nearby. After a few minutes of waiting, I rang the small silver bell on the counter, my knees knocking as the sound carried through the lobby. A couple of the tourists turned around to stare but quickly looked away when Mom scowled at them. Yikes.

The sound of inhumanely high heels ricocheted off the walls of the hotel as Cilia rounded the corner of the hallway to join us at the front desk. Spotting me standing there, she waved and slowed her stride, fixing her leather pencil skirt as she approached. "Hey, Addison." The witch looked over my shoulder at mom. "Sylvie! Good to see you again. It's been a while."

"Cilia Craven, my, my. You are a vision as always," Mother cooed. "Love what you did with the hair."

My friend patted her shoulder-length, wavy blonde bob, chuckling. "I needed a change," she said. "Though I might be going even shorter. You know what they say about getting over a breakup? Nothing works better to heal all wounds than self-care."

Wait, what? I hadn't realized Cilia and Sebastian broke up and she hadn't mentioned it before now. The two kept their relationship secret, which was understandable since Sebastian was a warlock. Witches and warlocks did not get along, and I assumed Cilia was waiting for the right time to go public in order to avoid any issues with her coven. But a breakup? That was news to me. For a moment, I wondered if I did anything to make it hard for Cilia to confide in me. We only recently started to get close and develop a friendship, but I would think she would feel comfortable telling me about a big life change.

Nerves ate away at me as I stood dumbfounded by the reception desk. Oblivious to my discomfort, Mom started spewing less than helpful advice on getting over a man, which made me cringe to listen to. I crooked a brow at Cilia, letting her know my surprise at hearing the news. Unable to interrupt my mother's monologue, the witch mouthed, "tell you later," before continuing to nod at whatever Mom said.

"So really, in the end, the only one who will ever love you is you," Mom finished.

Nausea shot up my throat and I fought the urge to start an argument. Maybe in Mom's life that was how it worked, but I didn't agree with the harsh sentiment.

I loved Gran with everything I had and I loved my wacky familiar as fiercely. As much as it scared me to admit it, my feelings for Joe were growing daily and I even had love left over for the mother who'd abandoned me without a second thought. There was plenty of love in my heart for everyone other than myself and I was certain the same people cared for me deeply in return. It made me sad that Mom didn't see things the way I did.

I wondered if it was part of what had pushed her away all those years ago.

"Are you two stopping in to say hi or...?" Cilia's face scrunched, and she tipped her head in Mom's direction.

I choked down a chuckle. "No, no. Mom doesn't need a room. She's still staying with me," I said, biting down on a snide comment. "I was hoping you could help me out."

"Oh?"

Glancing over my shoulder to make sure no one was listening, I leaned closer to Cilia. "What are the chances I could convince you to tell me if a certain person is staying in the hotel?" I asked.

The witch grimaced.

"I know, I know," I said, my arms up apologetically. "It's against the rules. I wouldn't ask if it wasn't important. Please, Cilia? I'd owe you one."

My friend sighed, looking at my mother. "How can I say no to that face?" she joked. "You can buy me a beer this weekend at the bar, for starters. And never speak of this again."

I nodded and whispered Tom's name in her ear so quietly I wasn't sure she heard me. As Cilia's eyebrows rose, I realized she had. Not only that, but she recognized Tom when I mentioned him. How?

"Why are you asking about him?"

"A hunch," I answered. "The less you know, the better. Trust me."

The witch sighed again but didn't make a move for the computer on the counter. Either Cilia had an incredible memory or I was right about her knowing Tom. Without bothering to check, she said, "He's here all right. Checked in three days ago and has an open reservation."

"That's quite the memory," my mother noted.

"Believe me, I never recall anything. Only reason I know about Sorrelis is because he's Isabella's special guest—" she wagged her manicured brows "—if you know what I mean."

Mom and I gasped in unison.

"Are you telling me your boss, the hot vampire boss woman, is dating a sleazy loan shark?" I asked.

Cilia's lips twitched. "Even better," she answered

in a hushed tone. "My vampire boss is getting frisky with a sleazy *warlock* loan shark."

Next to me, Mom's shrill laugh vibrated through the hotel lobby loud enough to get everyone's attention. Why on earth was Isabella Beaumont dating a warlock? Vampires did not mingle with other paranormals, especially not warlocks. The two species were the same level of stubborn with a touch of selfish, making them an unlikely pairing. What surprised me even more was that Isabella, who was more worthy of a woman crush than anyone else I knew, would stoop so low as to date a man that may very well be a murderer.

I continued to debate the relationship when Cilia said something that completely knocked my socks off.

"I'm surprised you haven't seen them together," my friend said. "They spend every morning at Bakes and Cakes. Aren't you usually there to pick up your order around that time?" Her cheeks heated. "Shoot, sorry, Piper. I forgot about Mrs. Cevil."

She continued to talk over herself, stumbling on her words, but I stopped paying attention. What Cilia said confirmed that Tom Sorrelis knew Mrs. Cevil, at least enough to frequent her bakery. And how did Isabella fit into all of this? My gut told me not to leave the bone alone, and I had to trust it. Adding the vampire to my list, I turned to Cilia and asked, "Think you can arrange for me to run into Tom somehow?"

"I'll do you one better," my friend said cheerfully. "Isabella left on a business trip this morning and I haven't seen him leave his room. If you promise to behave, you can drop off his lunch in my place."

I smiled. That, my friends, was why it was good to have friends in high places.

CHAPTER 11

The elevator shook and stopped; the door dinging to announce the third floor. My fingers curled over the handle of the food tray, knuckles white from the pressure. As the doors slid open, my stomach dropped.

Fear rising inside, I rolled the cart out of the elevator and stepped into the hallway of the hotel. To my left and right, a red carpet unrolled, leading to the rooms. At the end of each, gold frames hung on the walls with moody floral paintings inside. The darkness of the art was reminiscent of the emotions that swelled in my chest while I checked the plaque on the wall indicating the room numbers. In my pocket, my phone vibrated, and I took it out, relief washing over me as I read the message from Cilia.

"Your mom and I are here if you need us. Type SOS and we'll be there in a minute."

I wiped my brow, placing the phone on the cart where it was easy to reach. Anxiety rolled through me as I took the first step down the hallway. The cart wheels screeched with each turn, adding to the dreadful atmosphere. To my right, a bulb flickered in an ornate wall sconce and I jumped, my heart leaping into my throat.

"Get it together," I scolded myself. "It's not the first time you're doing this."

The pep talk did little to calm me down. While I had definitely bombarded people to get answers before, I hadn't felt so out of my depth then. Tom Sorrelis was a warlock and one whose magic I knew nothing about. Unlike witches, warlocks pulled their energy directly from the ley lines, so there was no telling how much power someone had until it was too late. For all I knew, Tom had recently replenished his energy source and considering my lame magic, he could easily take me out if things went south.

Then there was the matter of Isabella. I had no idea what the vampire was doing dating him but from what I knew, she wasn't someone to mess with. If she was spending time with Tom, he must be someone of magical value.

Unlike yours truly, who couldn't get a hold of her abilities no matter how much she tried.

I shivered, pushing the cart to a stop in front of the room Cilia mentioned. The smell of cheesy pasta wafted through the air and I noticed the small spill of coffee on the bleached white table cloth covering the tray. Great, I hadn't even knocked, and I already spilled the man's drink. He was never going to buy that I worked for the hotel.

Brushing out the wrinkles in my shirt with the palm of my hand, I shook out my wild curls and plastered a smile on my face. Then I knocked on the door.

"Who is it?" a low rumble of a voice sounded on the other side.

I breathed in, breathed out like Stella taught me in one of her torturous yoga lessons. "Lunch delivery!"

A shuffle of feet followed by a clearing of a throat had my knees knocking. I held on to the food tray for balance, spilling more coffee in the process. *Stop it!* I scolded myself. *You can do this.*

The door swung open, revealing a tall, slender man with eyes of sapphire and hair the color of night. Tom Sorrelis was an unconventional type of attractive. His long nose crooked at the tip and he had the showing of a five o'clock shadow on the bottom of his chin while the rest of his face remained clean-shaven. Because of his slim built, his cheekbones protruded from his skin in angular formations, drawing my attention back to his large eyes. He gave me a once over, his attention slowly shifting to the tray.

I slid a napkin over the coffee stain before he had the chance to notice.

"It smells wonderful," Tom said. His blue eyes landed on me, a wolfish grin forming. "Ah, a new face."

I stood up straighter. "Oh, yes," I said, extending a hand over the tray. "Piper Addison. I don't actually work for the Rose Hollow."

Reluctantly, the oil-slick of a man took my hand, shaking it briefly. A zap of electricity coursed through me as my magic sensed his. I swallowed hard, willing myself to relax. Before me, Tom's shoulders rolled as he looked me up and down and I gulped faster when the navy silk robe he wore started to part a little. I yanked my arm away, making him straighten up before I saw more of the warlock than I signed up for.

"And yet you are here to deliver my lunch," he said.

"I'm helping out a friend," I covered quickly.

The warlock tightened the belt of his robe and watched me suspiciously. On his right ring finger, a sparkle caught my eye, and I peeled my gaze away from him to glance down. A gaudy ring with a large blue stone in its center stared back at me. In my veins, my blood sizzled as my magic awakened again. My arm twitched, hand instinctively reaching for the jewelry. *His talisman,* I thought. I quickly tucked my hands behind my back before the electric current of my magic reared its shiny head.

Noticing me ogling him, Tom brought his hand higher, showing off the ring. "It's a family heirloom," he said, as though I didn't already know. "Great piece, isn't it?"

"Sure. Quite interesting," I lied. "Are you visiting Orchard Hollow?"

He nodded slowly. I was beginning to realize that everything Tom Sorrelis did was calculated; from the way he spoke to the way he'd purposefully answered the door in his robe, knowing it would make whoever was on the other side uncomfortable. He needed to be in control of every situation, and it made me dislike him even more.

I seriously did not understand Isabella's choice.

"I live a few towns over and am visiting on business," he said.

The killing kind? I sucked in a sharp breath before I said something I'd regret later. "What business are you in?"

"Finances. Small business loans, commercial investments, that type of thing."

Stabbing old ladies in the heart... My nostrils flared from anger and I had to pinch myself to keep from lashing out at the sleazeball. I had absolutely no proof that Tom killed Mrs. Cevil, but I couldn't stand the guy, regardless. The fact that he continued to stare at my chest while talking to me didn't help his case one bit. What a nasty piece of work.

I shook off my frustration and tried to get myself back on track. The conversation was starting to derail and Tom's lunch was getting cold. It wouldn't be long before he asked me to leave. Relaxing my stance, I feigned interest in his job and said, "Funny you should say that. I run my own business; the cafe across the street."

"You don't say?" the warlock cooed. His eyes lit up at the prospect of another sucker to add to his list of so-called clients. I stifled a groan as his lips peeled away from his teeth, giving him a sinister appearance. "Are you looking to invest?"

"Not unless I'm investing in a tray of freshly baked muffins," I replied. "My supplier is no longer in business so I'm in a bit of a bind. It's a tragic story. The woman was killed in her own bakery. Can you imagine?"

Tom's smile dropped. "You don't mean Reeba Cevil, do you?"

"You knew Mrs. Cevil?"

"I did, yes. She was a client," Tom said. I searched his face for a hint of guilt, but all I saw was surprise. If this slime bag killed Mrs. Cevil, he was fantastic at acting innocent. "When did it happen? The poor woman."

I was pretty sure the only thing the loan shark felt sorry for was his bank account getting slimmer.

"A few nights ago. You haven't heard anything about it? Her bakery was right down the street from here."

Tom scratched his over-gelled hair, his lips pursing. "I can't say I have. But then again, I'd been a little preoccupied."

The gleam in his eyes was back, and this time it wasn't for me. Nausea coated my mouth when I realized he was talking about spending time with Isabella. Were they together the night Mrs. Cevil was killed? I needed to find out.

Leaning in closer, I forced my face muscles to relax and said, "I don't mean to pry, but my friend mentioned you may be seeing Isabella Beaumont."

"Why does it matter?" Tom asked. A darkness cast over his face as he took a step back from me, his body settling into the dim light of his room.

"I'm sorry. I didn't mean to catch you off guard," I said as quickly as I could muster. "I was simply surprised. I've lived in Orchard Hollow my entire life and sometimes get caught up in the gossip. One of the most successful women in our town dating someone new doesn't go unnoticed."

At this, the warlock relaxed, his shoulders dropping slightly as he inched toward me. He hit the side of the food cart and his stupid robe parted once more. I averted my gaze immediately, suddenly finding the doorframe unbelievably interesting.

Tom chuckled, noticing my discomfort. "No need to be shy. I have nothing to hide," he said. *I bet you don't.* "And I do understand what you mean about small towns; I come from one myself."

"Right, you mentioned that earlier. How did you and Isabella meet if you don't mind me asking?"

"A business conference in Ridgewood," he replied. "She was the most beautiful woman there, so naturally I had to talk to her."

Naturally. Gross. My body screamed for me to get away from the creep, but I had more I needed to ask. Ridgewood... Why did that sound so familiar? I made a mental note to dissect the thought at a later time and returned my focus to the matter at hand. "You said Mrs. Cevil was a client," I said. "Did you happen to see her while you were visiting?"

"I sure did! Every morning at her bakery."

Hmm... exactly as Cilia said. It was beginning to look like Tom may not be as involved as I originally thought; if he was, why incriminate himself by telling me he was one of the last people to see Mrs. Cevil alive? It didn't add up. I scratched the back of my neck and breathed out the breath I was holding. Guilty or not, Tom was at the bakery often enough to notice anything out of the ordinary.

Blowing a stray hair out of my face, I studied the loan shark intently. "Did you notice anything strange with Mrs. Cevil when you last saw her?" I asked. "It was such a horrible death that I can't stop thinking about why someone would want to hurt a sweet old woman. I'm trying to make sense of it all."

"You know, I couldn't tell you," he said with a sigh. "As I mentioned, I was quite preoccupied with Bella. But if you're going to ask anyone, it should be the man she had helping out at the bakery. William. Last time I was there, they had a fairly loud argument. William ended up storming off and Reeba seemed pretty upset after."

Come again? Since when did Mrs. Cevil have a helper? As long as I knew her, she was a one woman act. It was the thing that impressed me most about her. Even at her age, she somehow managed to get every-thing done without breaking a sweat. Although now that I knew she was a witch, I was starting to believe magic had a bit to do with it.

Focus, Piper. Odd helper man. Stay with it.

I slapped myself mentally and said, "Did you see him at the bakery often?"

"Only a handful of times. Though Reeba mentioned it several times, she assumed it would make a difference to me somehow."

"Do you know what they may have argued about?"

"I'm afraid I don't," Tom said, his head shaking. "I'm also afraid my food must be cold by now."

Getting the hint, I promised Tom that I would have someone send a replacement meal and said my goodbyes. As I turned to walk away, the slimeball slipped me his business card with his personal cellphone number scribbled on it. "In case I needed someone to talk to," he said. What an absolute nightmare of a man.

On my way to the elevator, I tossed the business card in the trash and pressed the button seven times. I couldn't wait to get out of this hotel and away from Tom Sorrelis. While I no longer thought he had anything to do with Mrs. Cevil's murder, the man gave me the heebie-jeebies. *Really, Isabella? This guy?*

The doors slid open, and I walked inside, my reflection staring back at me in the large mirrored wall of the elevator. My eyes widened to orbs, a realization dawning on me.

I knew where I heard the name Ridgewood before. It was the city my mom said she last saw the Sisters of the River.

CHAPTER 12

After the hotel visit, mom decided to talk to a few local business owners on Cliff Row to catch up while I helped Rory with the post-lunch rush at the cafe. The steady flow of customers between one and three helped take my mind off the mess that had become my life, and I was grateful for it. It didn't matter how I spun it. This time, things were really getting out of hand.

Between my mother driving me nuts and taking over the farmhouse, Joe being gone with little availability for communication, and what happened to Mrs. Cevil, I was as lost as ever. All that without facing the gnawing doubt that stalked the mental door of my brain— what if Mom was right about what happened?

If she was, I was in more trouble than I thought. Mom guaranteed that the Sisters didn't know about my existence, that Malachi helped keep me hidden and that locking up my magic added an extra layer of protection against the coven. Yet I wasn't as convinced. Mrs. Cevil was working to bring the coven down, so if they figured out her plan, it wouldn't be long before they found out my mother's involvement. The discovery would surely lead them straight to our front door.

That is, if Mom's theory was true, which I still doubted it was.

At least that was what I told myself as I poured my twentieth cup of Gingerbread Latte and handed it to a customer without making eye contact. I was so lost in my own world; I didn't even hear my name being called. It wasn't until Rory casually smacked me with a wet rag as she passed by that I snapped out of it.

My head bounced up, eyes landing on a familiar face.

"Afternoon, Miss Addison," Sheriff Romero said. He snatched the latte from my hand and gave it a whiff, his eyes closing in satisfaction. "I sure need this today."

I topped up his cup when he sat it down. "Rough day at the office?"

"One way of putting it."

Romero brought the cup to his lips and downed half of it in one go. The foam from the latte mix stuck to the tip of his nose and I heard Rory chuckle from a few feet away. I deadpanned on the teenager, making her squirm and run off to the back to busy herself with something more important. Her cellphone, I assumed.

Not noticing the two of us, the sheriff continued to sip his drink while staring into space. A bead of sweat rolled down his brow and into his left eye without him even so much as twitching. Wow! He wasn't kidding about needing a coffee. Before he could object, I made a second latte and slid it across the counter toward him. "On the house," I said. "It seems you could use it."

The sheriff tipped the brim of his hat my way. "Thank you, Miss Addison. I appreciate the gesture."

"What has you in such a state?" I asked.

"You wouldn't believe me if I told you."

Snorting, I put my hands on my hips and whispered, "Witch, remember? Try me."

A shadow passed behind Romero's eyes as he checked the cafe for people. Seemingly satisfied with the few patrons who stood a ways away and weren't the least bit interested in our conversation, the sheriff took a tentative step toward me, his large hat obscuring most of my view.

"I really should not be telling you this, but it is so bizarre that I am having trouble believing it's real," he said, voice pitching.

My intrigue peaked. "What happened?"

"The body, Reeba's body, has been taken." The sheriff paused to look around again. "The undertaker called this morning to let us know."

The room spun around me and my vision narrowed. Black dots swarmed in my periphery as I tried to understand what the sheriff was saying. This had to be some sort of joke. I shook myself, clearing my throbbing head. "I'm sorry. Are you saying someone stole her dead body?"

"Precisely," the sheriff said.

"From the funeral home?"

His finger ran a circle around the rim of the coffee cup as he said, "Correct. It's the damnedest thing. In all my time as sheriff of this town, I never had anything so strange happen."

"What would anyone want with a dead body?"

"That is what I'm trying to find out," Romero said. "The undertaker is quite upset, but so far, we are yet to determine how someone got in and out of the funeral home without detection."

Reaching for the cold cup of coffee I'd been milking throughout the afternoon, I downed quickly, the caffeine helping my internal panic. "Do you think there was evidence on Mrs. Cevil's body that could lead to the killer?"

"It's possible," the sheriff said. "Mike, the coroner, is the most detail-oriented person I know, but even he can make a mistake. If there was something we missed, I doubt we'll find it now, even if we manage to recover the body."

As though coming out of a daze, the sheriff scrunched his nose, straightened his spine, and averted his eyes from me. He picked up his latte and topped it with a lid, his fingers turning white from the strength of his grip on it. I had the feeling he had said more than he believed he should have and while I didn't want him to get into any trouble at the station, I was glad to have the information. Mrs. Cevil's body was gone. Not gone, stolen.

This town was getting weirder by the minute.

The sheriff tapped his chin with his index finger and said, "I need to get back and clean up this mess. Thank you for the coffee, Miss Addison."

As he turned to leave, a clamor sounded in the office. I waved goodbye to the sheriff and hurried into the back, the door slamming shut behind me. The office was a mess. In the center, right in front of the desk, lay a pile of receipts I was supposed to organize for tax season later in the evening. On top of them, a collection of torn napkins spread in a thin layer of shredded paper and dust. My head swiveled to the right to see the supply shelf overturned, coffee beans and packets of sweetener spilling all over the floor.

Under the desk, a dozen marbles I had been collecting for a spell rolled around, their shiny surfaces reflecting the light streaming in from outside.

It looked like someone had broken in and vandalized the place, though the better part of me knew there was only one explanation for the disaster. My eyes flitted to the open alley door and the tiny muddy footprints leading from it to the stack of boxes in the corner.

"Harry Houdini!" I shouted. "How did you end up here and why?"

I was certain last I checked, the rascal was at the farmhouse causing his particular brand of havoc. Looking around the office, he must have been back here for hours. I really needed to find out how the raccoon managed to get from place to place before he destroyed every part of my life with his chaotic nonsense.

"Spring cleaning?"

Heart in my throat, I spun around to watch Stella

float toward me, circling around the pile of paperwork on the floor. Her tennis skirt fluttered behind her as the ghost picked up speed to stand beside me.

I groaned. "Is it me or is Harry suddenly extra mobile?"

"He definitely gets around," my familiar said.

"Seriously, how does he manage to move through town so easily? I swear I saw him at the house this morning before I left."

In answer, Stella pointed to the stack of boxes and the bushy tail sticking out from them. She pointed a gray finger toward it. "As my dear husband always said, if you want answers, go straight to the source."

Winking at my familiar, I wiggled my fingers and pushed my magic to the surface. Shockingly, it obliged immediately. Even my magic wanted to teach Harry a lesson. I tiptoed to the boxes he hid behind, careful to keep my feet from landing too hard so as not to scare him off until I was ready. When I was a few feet away, I looked at Stella over my shoulder, waited for her thumbs up, then zapped the box closest to me. The lightning on my fingers flashed, hitting the box and making it topple sideways. The sound of my magic slamming into a solid object echoed through the office and even Stella yelped as the box fell to the ground.

Behind it, Harry stirred lazily. His hind legs

stretched and as I peered over the box, I realized he was lying on his back; coming out of a nap. The raccoon's eyes flashed wide when he saw me towering over him and he grabbed an object off the ground, clutching it close to his chest as he tried to roll over.

It worked in my favor that Harry's exercise routine was worse than mine and it took forever for him to right himself, giving me enough time to leap toward him and snatch the item out of his paws. At first, I thought it might be a cookie since those were his favorite treats, but after the last time he got into one of my potions and nearly died, I wasn't taking any chances.

It wasn't until I had the small object in my hands that I realized my mistake. While the thing I held was of the magical variety, it wasn't one of mine.

"What is it?" Stella yelled out from behind the desk.

At my feet, Harry hissed at her and a long string of curse words escaped my familiar. I pushed the box with my foot to put a wall between them and turned to Stella. "Protection charm," I told her, dangling the leather pouch in the air. Inside the pouch, the sound of crystals bouncing around pierced the air and the smell of cinnamon and rosemary wafted up my nose, confirming my assessment. I dug my finger in to pull out a chain with a fuchsia, talon-shaped crystal on its end. "Against vampire compulsion. Where do you think he found it? It's not mine."

"Rory?"

I disagreed. "She's practicing the basics," I said. "This spell work is much too advanced for her."

As the chain swung back and forth before me, an engraving on its rear caught my attention. I brought the talon closer, inspecting the tiny letters stamped into the silver clasp around the crystal. My jaw hung open.

"R.C."

"What's that?"

Beckoning Stella closer, I waited until she vanished and re-materialized beside me to show her what I discovered. "You don't think..." I scratched my chin. "Reeba Cevil. Could Harry have found a way into the bakery and found this there?"

"It's possible. He certainly loved the scones that are no longer here."

I brought the crystal to my nose, pulled apart the strings and gave it a good whiff. There was no mistaking it— this was a charm against compulsion. But why did Mrs. Cevil have it? Since humans couldn't manipulate the mind, she must have spelled it against a paranormal. Few of my kind possessed the magic to alter someone's perception. Warlocks were able to tap into the ability with enough power, but it usually required a lot of energy, so most of them stayed away from the process. That only left one possibility.

A vampire.

My thoughts jumbled as I recalled the odd feeling I got when Tom mentioned where he met Isabella. Could it have been a coincidence that she visited Ridgewood? Perhaps. Yet now that I held a compulsion charm in my hands, I was thinking otherwise.

What I needed was Joe. If anyone could help me brainstorm through this, it was another vampire—specifically one that knew Isabella Beaumont. We were supposed to have another call tonight after dinner and I added asking him about the charm to my growing list of things to do. Until then, there was another task I had on my mind.

I eyed my familiar. Stella was the perfect candidate to help me with it.

"Oh no..." she said, seeing the mischievous gleam in my eyes. "You're up to something."

I chuckled. "I sure am. Meet me in the car."

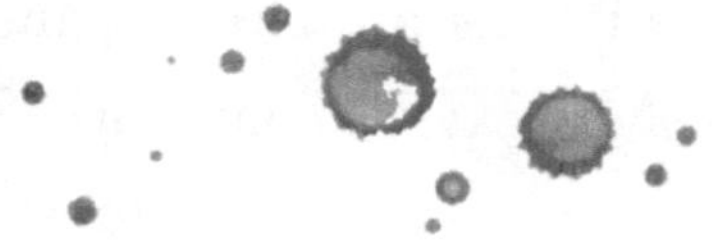

Mistbrook Manor sat at the top of a hill nestled between a long ridge of mountains and a hard dropoff to the sea. As I wove the car up the winding driveway leading to the funeral home, a sense of dread racked my body. I didn't know what I expected to find here, but the place gave me the chills.

We passed through thick iron gates with thorny vines climbing up the side columns; the name of the manor curved above in old gothic letters. I shivered, my fingers holding strong on the wheel.

"Spooky place," Stella remarked.

I had to agree. The funeral home had always given me a feeling of unease and it wasn't because of the dead bodies inside. The entire area repelled me, as though it screamed for me to leave as soon as I was near it. I had never had to set foot inside, luckily. When Gran died, she was clear that she wanted to be cremated and for it to be handled briskly by the hospital morgue one town over. Now that I was here, I wondered if it was more for my benefit than hers. To spare me from coming here.

We reached the front of the manor and I parked the car off to the side, as far away from the main entrance as possible. If I had to describe the house rising tall before me, I would say it was as monstrous as it was beautiful. The three-story black brick Victorian manor was taller than it was wide, making it appear to be reaching high to the sky with scaly fingers. There was a small porch in front with two rose bushes on either side of the steps, both of which were in full bloom with stunning red flowers. In the center of the porch sat a red door that perfectly matched the color of the roses.

Two bay windows framed the entrance, both with dark curtains drawn shut. On the second floor, three more windows with black shutters stared at me like wobbly eyes. Above them was the attic and a twisty, iron weathervane that creaked as it spun in the wind.

Yikes.

I turned over my shoulder to find Stella. "Ready?"

"I go in and look around while you distract the undertaker?"

Nodding, I took a tentative step up, then another. Soon I was at the front door and quaking in my boots. Wind trilled in my ear as my familiar ghosted me, literally. While Stella did her thing inside, I had to keep up with my part and be the bait. My hand rose to knock and stopped when I spotted the bronze sign hanging right below the old-school knocker.

"Please call for an appointment."

Great. I shook my head, frustrated. Who made appointments in this place? Not like it was a spa. Lowering my hand, I spun on my heel and sat down on the stairs to wait for Stella's return. I could only hope the undertaker didn't come out to see me sitting here. Talk about a stalker.

Leaning back on my elbows, I rolled my gaze over the grounds of Mistbrook Manor, trying to imagine what the place was like before it became the home of the dead. I could picture a steady inflow of guests coming in and out, parties the best of the best attended, and laughter as children ran around the front yard playing. From what Gran told me, the manor used to be the family home of a prominent family in town. As time wore on, members died and moved away, leaving it mostly abandoned. As far as I knew, the woman who owed it now, the undertaker, kept to herself and stayed out of the town's business. A fitting personality trait for someone in her profession.

A flash of movement dragged me from my thoughts. My head jerked up, eyes narrowing on the massive oak tree sitting on the edge of the cliff not far from the manor. For a second, I thought I saw a woman duck behind the tree, her arm stretched as if to call me forward. She was too far away to make out any features, but she was there, I was certain of it.

I stood up and walked down the steps slowly. Glancing at the front door, I made my way toward the tree, my heart hammering in my chest. Teeth chattering, I gathered my courage and skirted around the trunk.

Nothing.

I glanced to the left and right, but there was not a soul in sight.

"Weird," I whispered. I was sure I saw someone.

"Hey!"

My heart skidded up my chest and I bit my tongue hard enough to draw blood. Hands gripping the tree trunk, I caught my wavering breath, eyes focusing on Stella standing tall before me. "For the love of! Stop that!"

"What are you doing over here?" the ghost asked, looking at the sea beyond us. "Sightseeing?"

I waved her off. "Nothing. I thought I saw someone. How did it go?"

"Total bust," Stella answered. "No one was there and when I checked the morgue, nothing appeared out of place. I even checked for runes like you asked and couldn't find a thing. Whoever snatched your body knew what they were doing."

"Wonderful."

Stella's large lips pouted, making them appear large than life. "Don't sweat it," she told me. "You'll find something soon. You usually do."

Somehow, I doubted it. It seemed that this time around, the mystery I'd got myself involved in was too tough to crack. No matter which way I spun it, I could not make sense of why someone would want Mrs.

Cevil dead. Even Mom's theory was looking thin and I hated to admit that it was the only one we had left.

I checked my watch, realizing for the first time how late it was. Waving to get Stella's attention, I turned around and headed back to the car, deflated. Perhaps Joe could shed some light on the situation. Right now, he was my only hope.

CHAPTER 13

Kicking Mom out of the house so that I could have a night off was easier than I imagined it would be. I didn't even have to try. Actually, it was Sylvie's idea she head out for the evening to give me a break from having her around. An oddly in-tune notion from her. I should have been worried about what she may be up to—considering how little she was willing to share about her plans— but I was desperate for a quiet evening. And a proper chat with Joe, if I were being honest.

As soon as Mom was out the door, I got to work. It'd been a few days since I saw Joe and I really wanted to make a good impression on our video call this evening. Despite Stella's protests, I opted out of washing my "fit for a mental institution" hair, her words, not mine, and put it up in a loose bun instead. For my outfit, I chose an oversized sweater that fell off my shoulder and added a touch of sparkle with a vintage crystal necklace I found in Gran's jewelry box. I even put on makeup to take away the bags under my eyes.

By the time eight o'clock rolled around, I was ready.

Opening a bottle of merlot, I settled in on the couch in front of a lit fireplace and propped my laptop up on the coffee table. Joe was late. The vampire's timing had often been impeccable and for a brief moment, I thought I was being stood up. When my computer dinged to signal an incoming call, the wine I had taken a sip of rushed down my throat and I coughed up a lung before finally accepting. The screen lit up and Joe's face stared back at me. He had a slight beard today and it accentuated the sharp edges of his cut jaw. His green eyes carried the weight of a storm as he looked me over, one corner of his lips ticking up.

Oh my coffee... I sure missed the man.

"Hey, you," Joe said. He looked around the living room as though searching for something. "Sylvie not there?"

A smile escaped me. "Shockingly, she excused herself for my benefit. How are you? Everything all right in the city?"

"I hope to be wrapping up here soon," Joe replied. "It's a tougher case than I originally thought. I'll explain more when I'm back, but let's say that I do not miss this part of the job."

Prior to buying his uncle's bookstore, Brooks Books, and moving to Orchard Hollow, Joe was a big shot lawyer in King City. From what he told me, the pressure of the job got to him, and he needed a fresh start. When his uncle passed away and the shop went up for sale, he took it as a sign. Unlike me, Joe settled into his own here quite quickly. It helped that Brooks Books was the only bookshop in town that catered to a more eclectic clientele of the paranormal variety. If you had magic, the shop was the place to go to get information on new spells, the ley lines, the history of our kind; pretty much anything you could imagine. For the humans who knew nothing about our existence, the shop offered a fun selection of occult books that drew in a decent crowd come tourist season.

All in all, Joe loved the slower paced life in Orchard Hollow much better and I was grateful I got to meet him.

I brought the glass to my lips, relaxing into the

couch cushions. "Hopefully you can wrap up soon and head home," I said. "We miss you around here."

"Assuming you're talking about Stella and Harry?" he teased.

"Definitely," I said with a chuckle. "The raccoon has been crying out your name in his sleep. You might want to drive over ASAP."

Joe raked his fingers through his hair, his gaze following the movement of the glass at my lips. "Anyone else missing me in town?"

My cheeks burned with a fire of a thousand suns. I tried to finish my drink but either my mouth and brain refused to talk to each other, or I had forgotten how drinking works because next thing I knew the merlot was running down my chin. Horrified, I wiped it away with the sleeve of my sweater, hoping Joe didn't notice it. If he did, he made no move to mention it.

"Nancy Steeles made a few comments about the bookstore being closed," I said, my brain working overtime to erase the last few seconds. "And it's possible there's another witch that wishes you weren't so far away."

"Glad to hear it."

Joe winked, and my whole body shuddered. *Keep it together. Jeez.*

To spare me further embarrassment, he changed the subject, asking, "How goes the snooping?"

"I'm not snooping!"

My boyfriend— maybe sort of boyfriend— looked at me through hooded eyes, his one brow arching higher. I groaned. "Okay, fine! I may be doing a little bit snooping. But wouldn't you be if the tables were reversed?" I asked. "I'm glad you called because I wanted to run something by you."

"Oh?"

"I'm in a bit of a spot," I admitted. "Some things have come to light, and it's as though I have a theory on the tip of my tongue, but I can't quite put it together. I was thinking if we talk it out like we used to, it might help."

Joe's warm smile made me melt further until I was one with the couch I sat on. "Go for it," he said. "Hopefully I can help."

For the next hour, I proceeded to fill Joe in on everything I had uncovered thus far. I didn't leave anything out. Not my lack of trust in my mother, not the mysterious disappearance of the body, not even the woman I thought I saw at the funeral home. Joe listened patiently, letting me indulge in my monologue until my mouth was dry from speaking and the words started to get tangled together. When it came time to tell him about Isabella Beaumont, I paused.

"What is it?" Joe asked, sensing my hesitation.

Clearing my throat, I leaned my elbows on my

knees and looked him in the eyes. "There's another thing that came up that could be important but could be nothing," I said. "It's about Isabella Beaumont."

"Piper, I thought I told you before to steer clear of her," Joe warned.

I put my hands up defensively. "I know, I know. Nothing good comes from pushing a vampire," I repeated his words to him. "Except you, of course."

"It's because of who I am that I know who to stay away from."

"So you admit she could be involved somehow," I noted. "It's odd for her to be in the exact city the Sisters were last operating out of, isn't it? I mean, what even happens in Ridgewood?"

Joe bit his bottom lip hard. "According to Tom Sorrelis, business conferences."

"Yes, sure, you're right. It's probably a coincidence."

"I'm not saying it is," Joe corrected. "All I'm saying is if Isabella is somehow involved with the Sisters of the River and they're the ones who killed your baker, you need to be more careful. From what you've told me, this is an immensely powerful coven that managed to stay under the radar for a long time. You don't want to cross witches that strong."

I started to speak when Joe added, "And you don't want to cross Isabella. Trust me."

"Is there anything you want to tell me?" I asked. "About the two of you?"

Joe smirked. "Nothing of that sort. Our paths crossed in another life and believe me when I tell you, Isabella may look innocent, but she is far from it."

Were we talking about the same woman here? I had never pegged Isabella Beaumont to be innocent. Fierce with a run-you-over-if-you-look-at-me-wrong attitude. Sure, but innocent? Not even close. The more Joe said, the more I started to think that there was a story he wasn't sharing, one that I desperately wanted to find out.

Yet I couldn't force him. After I found out Joe was a vampire, I avoided him like the plague. Any other man would have walked away a long time ago, but not Joe. He stuck around, and he was patient and kind; he waited for me to be ready to be his friend. Then he waited for more. As Stella would say, he was a fine catch, and I'd be dumb to mess it up. Except she'd say it in a more colorful language.

If a time came when Joe was ready to share his history with Isabella, I'd listen. Until then, it was best to respect his privacy and leave it alone.

I had other things to worry about, anyway.

"What would you do next if you were me?"

"Walk away and never think of Mrs. Cevil again?" Joe suggested. I shrugged. "I had to try. If I were in your place, and I still firmly believe you should let things go, but knowing you by now, I doubt you will, I'd try to locate William next."

My ears perked up. "Of course! Mrs. Cevil's so-called helper that I never knew she had. The one Tom mentioned."

"Yes, him," Joe said. "If anyone could give you information on who frequented the bakery and who may have wanted to harm Mrs. Cevil, it would be the guy who was behind the scenes. You might get lucky."

I thought about what he said, agreeing that it was the best course of action. "Now all I need is his last name and address."

"Have you thought about calling in a favor?" Joe asked.

"I already asked Romero for one," I replied. "He won't do any more for me."

Joe's head shook, his messy hair falling into his eyes. He blew the strands away, saying, "I'm not referring to the sheriff. You need a tracker."

I didn't understand at all. Joe couldn't have been referring to anyone on the police force because otherwise, he would have said so. Who else? It must have been a paranormal, but the only species that was known for their tracking abilities were werewolves and I didn't...

My thoughts cut off. Of course! If I wanted to track William, a werewolf was my best bet. Everyone knew they could pinpoint a person's location based on their scent alone. All I needed was to get a werewolf into Bakes and Cakes to have them analyze the lingering scents.

And I knew just the werewolf for the job.

"Ember Mint," I whispered. "Oops, Crowley."

"Uh-huh. She certainly owes you one for putting her husband behind bars and getting her that hefty divorce settlement."

How could I have forgotten? It seemed forever ago that I helped the sheriff solve Daniel Tse's case. If it weren't for me butting my nose in where it didn't belong, no one would ever know that Ember's cheating ex-husband was the one who killed the warlock for his mistress. And Ember was the only female werewolf in our town, if not the country, so she'd probably help me out. Girl power and whatnot.

My resolve strengthened and my spirits lifted. I spent the rest of the evening having a much lighter conversation with Joe until both our eyes were too tired to stay open. Wishing him goodnight, I dragged my tired behind up the stairs and fell into my bed, giddy with the thought of getting further on the case tomorrow.

I was so exhausted, I didn't even question how quiet the house was. As my eyes closed, I briefly wondered why Mom wasn't back yet, but within seconds, sleep took me and the thought vanished into nothingness.

CHAPTER 14

Sitting on the bench outside of the Orchard Hollow Pharmacy in the early morning and nursing my third cup of coffee made me feel like an absolute creep. Not that I could help it; if I wished to talk to Ember, this place was my best bet to catch her. The thing about Ember Crowley was she wasn't just the female werewolf in our town, she was also our only pharmacist and owner of a very successful drugstore on Cliff Row. All that to say, Ember was on a lady boss level I couldn't even imagine.

A tiny flake of snow landed on my forehead. I brushed it off, my nose twitching from the cold. The trickling of snow indicated that holidays were around the corner and I was yet to finalize the cafe's festive menu. I looked at the intricate miniature town in the pharmacy window, deflating. Another thing Ember was better at than me. It was a wonder I managed to keep the cafe afloat considering how little time I'd been spending in it lately.

I shook the negative thoughts off, reminding myself that Ember didn't stumble on dead bodies everywhere she turned.

"Piper?"

I looked up to see Ember's lean frame tower over me, then glanced at my watch. Six fifteen, right on schedule. The werewolf's messy bob fell into her face and she fixed it back into place effortlessly, her dark eyes squinting. Smiling, I fixed my coat and stood up. "Hey, Ember. I was hoping to run into you. How's it going?"

"Good, good," the werewolf said as she attempted to read me for clues. "Are you here about a prescription? Because I don't open until nine."

"Oh, nothing like that," I said. "I need a favor. But it might be better to talk in private."

Unbuttoning her long wool jacket to reveal a crisp white lab coat with only a thin tee under it, Ember nodded to the door and after several clicks of two sets of keys, let me inside. I kept my coat on, not wanting to waste her entire morning with my presence. Also, because it was the coldest day we'd had so far and, unlike Ember, I didn't have werewolf blood coursing through my veins. Everyone knew her kind ran hot no matter what the surrounding temperature was.

Following her inside, I tried not to cringe at the obscene amount of Christmas decorations set up throughout the pharmacy. One quirk of Ember's was her obsession with all things Christmas, a fact she made known by keeping them up almost all year round. Seriously, I once saw her decorate a garland in August. It was bizarre.

I kept my arms tucked into my sides as we walked to avoid knocking over the Santa figurines stashed on the shelves. Nestled between bottles of ointments and boxes of Band-Aids, they seemed to reach for me as I passed, and my body recoiled from them instinctively. Werewolf or not, Ember was odd like the rest of us, a notion that brought me a tiny joy as I followed the tall woman to the back of the pharmacy.

Reaching the rear, Ember dropped her coat on the waiting area bench and pointed to the small room behind the dispensary counter. "Coffee?"

I looked at the cup in my hands.

"I mean one more," Ember corrected, laughing.

"No, thank you. I'm going straight into work after this, so I'm sure I'll have plenty there." Feeling embarrassed I didn't bring a latte for her, I added, "I can come back with one of our Gingerbread drinks for you later if you want."

The werewolf glanced between me and the coffee machine in the small kitchenette behind her. "Sure," she said. "That sounds much better than what I have going on around here. Thank you. So, how can I help?"

Suddenly, the words I had practiced a million times on the way over evaporated from my brain. It was one thing to question Ember about her ex-husband the way Joe and I had done earlier in the year; we needed to get information only she could provide us with. Asking a paranormal to use their magical abilities to help you when you've never interacted with them on a friendly basis before was quite another. Especially when that paranormal was a werewolf, they were more secretive about their magic than the rest of us.

I tore at a hangnail, nerves hammering against my chest.

"Okay, please tell me to leave if you think I'm overstepping," I said. Why did I start with that statement? Sometimes I really disliked myself. Gulping, I started over. "What I mean is, I am hoping you can help, but it's a delicate matter."

Ember's eyes narrowed on me.

"I'm not explaining very well, am I?" I asked.

"I'm afraid you're not explaining at all."

Gathering my thoughts once more, I tried again. This time, I forgot all about paranormal codes of conduct and my own foolishness. Instead, the only thing I had on the forefront of my mind was Mrs. Cevil. I couldn't let her killer get away, not if there was anything I could do about it. I stretched my lips into a smile, though it was likely closer to a grimace. "Mrs. Cevil from Bakes and Cakes down the street was killed and I'm trying to find out what happened. Don't ask why, I'm unclear on that myself. Unfortunately, I am at a dead end."

"Oh," Ember said. For a moment, I thought she was going to laugh in my face for the word vomit I threw her way, but she ended up surprising me. Returning my grimace-smile, she said, "I heard about Reeba. It's a real tragedy. I'm happy to help any way I can, but I have to admit, we weren't friends or anything."

Really? Was everyone on the street on a first name basis with Mrs. Cevil except me? No matter. Shaking off my wayward thoughts, I concentrated on Ember. "I know you didn't know her well. That's not why I'm here. I need to locate a person, someone who worked for Mrs. Cevil and it might require—" I paused to swallow the saliva pooling in my mouth "—your special brand of abilities."

"This thing?" Ember asked, pointing to the tip of her nose.

I laughed. "That's the one," I replied. "If it's not too much to ask, of course. His name is William, but that's all I have. I can probably get something from the bakery that would have his scent, but it might be easier if I found a way to get you inside instead."

Ember's head cocked to the side, and she gave me a once over before turning on her heels and marching into the kitchenette. As she waltzed away, panic rose inside me and tried to claw its way out. Have I offended her? Did I overstep?

My mind was reeling the entire time she was gone, and by the time the werewolf returned with a file folder in hand, I was a puddle of nerves. Handing me the folder, Ember flashed her pearly whites and said, "Here you go."

Wait, what? Confusion rose to the surface as I tried to understand what had happened. My grimy fingers reached for the folder and when I opened it, I wanted to shriek. If I were being honest, I wanted to hug Ember, but I was pretty certain forcing yourself on a werewolf was a one-way street to getting your butt kicked. Especially this close to a blood moon.

"You have his home address," I said, eyes scanning the printout in the folder Ember handed to me. My gaze flicked the black-and-white photo of a man in his early thirties. He had curly blond hair that was cut short to his scalp, and a distinct scar running across one of his bushy brows. "And his picture."

"Sure do," Ember replied. "William Prude has had asthma since he was a kid. He and his mother, Evelyn, have been customers for years. I'm probably breaking every code in the book giving you his file, but I owe you one."

That's what I was hoping for...

I grinned like an idiot. "Thank you, Ember. Honestly, I won't forget this." A rogue tear crept into my left eye, and I swiped it away. "I know you're risking a lot to help me. I wouldn't ask if it wasn't important."

"Don't mention it," Ember said. "Reeba and I weren't best friends, but it's awful what happened to her. If I can help in any way, I'm happy to do it. And you know what they say, we have to stick together."

She winked.

"Definitely," I agreed. I jammed the folder into my purse and turned to leave, saying, "I'll pop in with that latte soon. And again, thank you so much!"

As I bolted for the front door, a lightness in my step carried me forward. Finally, things were working out. I had a name and an address— a new direction. Talking to William might prove to be useless, but for all I knew, he saw the person who hurt Mrs. Cevil.

Most people around here didn't pay attention to others, I knew this from experience in my own cafe. Heck, I never even knew Mrs. Cevil had someone helping out, and I'd been coming to the bakery since I opened the business. Perhaps the killer visited the bakery prior to Mrs. Cevil's death and William saw them.

I had to hope that was the case because I was running out of options.

A rogue thought gnawed at the back of my mind as I speed-walked down the street toward the cafe. Mom still hadn't returned from her night out. Before she left, she told me not to wait up and this wouldn't be the first time the woman partied too hard to come home. I was starting to get worried about her. Between the murder, her determination that the Sisters of the River were to blame, and what I saw in the greenhouse, I wasn't so sure of Mom's safety.

Perhaps Rory could hold down the fort after the morning rush so I could run over and check the farmhouse to see if she returned.

My steps faltered as I neared the front door of Bean Me Up. It was too early for any business to be open yet, so when I saw two people outside the door, I had to do a double take. Nestled in the entranceway of the cafe stood my mother. She was wearing the same purple dress she had on the night before, the one that showed off too much of her cleavage for my comfort. Her head was tilted back in a laugh and she had her arm looped under the arm of a tall man half her age. I stifled a gasp when I saw the blond turn around to face me, the scar on his brow standing out against his pale features.

She didn't!

"Hi, honey," my mother said as I approached. "Have you met William Prude?"

CHAPTER 15

Sylvie Addison

I was a terrible mother. All right, maybe not the absolute worst, but if you listened to my daughter, you'd think I deserved an award. I knew Piper wanted me out of the house and out of her life even though she never said it. One thing about my girl was she was always easy to read, what with her expressive face and even more expressive mouth. Mom said she took after me in that way, but heaven forbid Piper ever admit we were anything alike.

Joke's on her— stubbornness was another thing we had in common.

I watched anxiety pour off her as she came

through the door, my heart sinking at the thought of having caused it. Sure, I didn't kill poor Reeba, but my presence in Orchard Hollow was taking a toll on Piper and I felt terrible for intruding on her life. As much as I hated to admit it, Piper and I were nothing more than strangers now. Mostly because of my own actions.

I wished there was a way to make her understand why I had to leave, why it was the only way to protect her from those vicious, bloodthirsty witches. And from him.

She'd never buy it.

Keeping her in the forefront of my mind, I told Piper I was stepping out for a wild night in town so she could have some space for herself and the privacy she desperately craved. She'd likely spend it chatting up the handsome vampire, my opinion of whom had not yet been fully formed. Regardless, she needed time alone, and I had a lead to follow.

Taking a final glance at my beautiful daughter, I zipped up Mom's old faux-fur jacket I'd found in the attic and stepped outside. The wind was furious this time of year and the trees surrounding our slice of heaven had already shed their leaves. Their corpses taunted me as I made the brisk walk down the driveway to meet the taxi driver. Settling into the leather seats, I let my head loll to the side, a much needed catnap taking control of my tired body.

I awoke with a start, the taxi stopping in a familiar part of town. Paying the man with the last of my petty cash, I stepped out and inhaled the cold night air. My lungs froze taking it in, but I stood steady, knowing that once I leave, I would miss this part of Orchard Hollow. Despite what Piper thought, I'd actually liked it here once upon a time.

My eyes drifted to the piece of paper in my hands. "Prude..." I whispered into the busy parking lot of the Cliffside Diner. The name sounded familiar, but I couldn't quite place it. Still, it drew me in and I felt I needed to investigate further, if only to give my daughter a break.

While Piper was busy tearing apart Reeba's life to find a lead, I knew better. The Sisters killed my friend; there was no doubt in my mind about it. Now all I needed was the chance to prove it to my headstrong daughter so she would pack her bags and get the hell out of Dodge before it was too late. Not yet though. She wasn't ready and there was much to do before she was strong enough to go up against him.

I shuddered, pulling the jacket tighter around me. Piper had to win this, she just had to. If there was anything I'd taught my daughter before I left, it was how to survive and goddess help me I would make sure she got through this unharmed.

Or all of us would pay the price...

I shook my head and took the first step toward the diner, where I knew Reeba's handyman would be. I'd never met the man, but she spoke highly of him, often mentioning him on our weekly calls. William this and William that. If he wasn't young enough to be her grandson, I'd think they had a thing going. Another shiver racked my spine, and I sped up my pace to get inside. The major bonus of listening to the witch go on and on about a random person fixing her pipes— the literal ones— was how much I had gotten to know about William without ever seeing him. For example, I knew he'd be at the Cliffside Diner trying to find his next wife on Thursday night.

Smoothing down my frizzy hair, I pulled down the low-cut collar of my dress and opened the door. The sound of jazz surrounded me and I floated into the restaurant, my hips swaying as I walked. Eyes followed my every move as I sauntered up to the bar, the silk skirt draping long behind me. No one I needed to concern myself with. There was only one man whose attention I craved, and I was yet to spot him. I pulled out a chair, the slit in my skirt parting to allow too much of my leg to be exposed. Exactly as I planned it.

Out of the corner of my eye, I noticed a gray fox make his way toward me and glowered. If it were any other time, I'd entertain the idea of speaking to the man, but not tonight. I was on a mission. Positioning myself away from him, I called the bartender over and ordered my own drink, something I hadn't done in ages. Luckily, the fox got the clue and continued to walk past me, the disappointment on his face evident for all to see. My lips quirked into a smile.

Still got it.

A glass of whiskey on ice slid toward me and I was about to pay when a deep voice sounded behind me.

"Put it on my tab," a voice said.

I turned slowly, interested to see who was so bold as to assume I wished to speak to him. As I twisted, excitement fluttered in my belly. My cheeks dimpled as I inspected the tall glass of handsome before me. Blond hair, curly and neatly trimmed. Piercing brown eyes with a touch of gold around the edges. A scar that ran across one brow in such a precise manner, I'd think it was purposefully cut.

Perfection.

I extended an arm, letting my fingers idle on the man's hand when he took it. "Sylvie Addison," I said, my voice a song. "And you are?"

"William Prude," he replied.

Like I didn't already know.

My grin never faltered as I pulled out the empty chair beside me. "Pleasure to meet you, William. Care to join me?"

CHAPTER 16

To say I was surprised to find my mother cozying up to William Prude in the doorway of Bean Me Up was the understatement of the century. What was she thinking? The woman was in town all of two seconds and her love life was already more eventful than mine had been in the last forty-plus years living here. Excluding the past few months with Joe, of course. More importantly, though, was why William? How was my mother one step ahead of me having not lifted so much as a finger to investigate Mrs. Cevil's death?

Unless I was completely wrong about what she'd been doing the last few days.

An image of the dark magic Mom cast in the

greenhouse popped in my head and I shook it off. I couldn't let myself go there. Mom wouldn't kill someone she said was her friend... would she?

I peered over the espresso machine at the two love-birds canoodling at the table near the window. There really was no way to tell what the woman was capable of.

The machine whirred to life, and I continued to watch Mom and William while I waited for the espresso to pour. My hand twirled the milk jug, frothing it for much longer than was necessary. Each second that passed was one more second I didn't have to interrupt the gross display of affection they had going on. The one bonus of growing up without a father was that I never had to see whatever this was in front of me. No matter what they tell you, nothing prepared you for watching your Mom flirt.

I swallowed the nausea circling in my stomach and poured the milk into three large cups. The smell of coffee and gingerbread floated through the air, temporarily making me forget where I was. If only I could stay back here forever.

As if sensing my reluctance to join them, my mother broke away from William long enough to yell, "What's the holdup, honey? Do you need help?"

I think you're helping enough. Flashing a thumbs up, I stacked the cups onto a tray and waddled over to their table, checking the clock above the door as I did. We had twenty minutes before I had to open the cafe. Too short to get any proper questioning done and yet much too long if I had to endure another moment of hearing Mom's fake laugh.

"These smell absolutely divine," Mom said, grinning.

"Yes, wonderful," William agreed. He never took his eyes off her and I tried not to gag in my mouth. Whatever Mom was doing, it was working.

Careful not to betray how I truly felt about the coupling, I picked up a cup and held it for emotional support as I slid into an empty chair. "So," I said, gesturing between them. "How did this come about?"

A foot jabbed me under the table. I flinched, catching Mom's sharp eyes. Point noted. I shifted in my seat, sipping on the latte before it got cold. "What I meant to ask is, how did you two meet?" I corrected.

"Well, it was the darndest thing," William explained. "I was at the Cliffside Diner having a nightcap when out of nowhere the most gorgeous woman I had ever laid eyes on walked in. I knew right there and then that I absolutely had to speak to her."

"And I was more than happy to oblige," my mother cooed.

Ew. Untwisting my face, I avoided Mom's gaze when I said, "I take it this was last night?"

"Uh-huh," William nodded. "Haven't made it home yet."

Double ew.

There was not enough coffee in the world to erase the interaction from my memory. I wished I could scrub my brain clean like I would a dirty apron, but unfortunately that wasn't in the cards for today. The point was further burned into my psyche as Mom dragged an agonizingly slow finger over William's forearm.

Seriously, I was going to lose my lunch at any moment.

Keeping my features as neutral as I could despite the fresh hell I landed in, I straightened the curve of my back and dimpled my cheeks. "You know, William," I said in a honeyed tone. "You look very familiar."

"Honey, don't you recognize him from Reeba's?" Mom asked. Her eyes jumped ever so slightly, the only indication that she wanted me to play along. "He helps out at the bakery with the odds and ends."

I licked my lips. "You don't say..."

Sitting between us, William was completely clueless. If I didn't think he had impure intentions toward my mother, I'd have felt sorry for the guy. Mom was playing him like a fiddle and he was none the wiser.

"I used to help out," he said awkwardly. "Not sure what to do with myself now."

And like that, I had an in.

Mom's eyes widened, and she tilted her head to the side, motioning for me to get moving. I peeled my gaze away from her before I blew it. "I'm so sorry to hear about Mrs. Cevil," I told William. "Were you two good friends?"

He shook his head, his eyes on the table. Next to him, Mom's hand lifted to rest on his and she gave him a tiny squeeze of reassurance. My heart jolted. I really missed the way she used to make everything better simply by being there.

"We spent a lot of time together," William answered, putting an end to my trip down memory lane. "Me being in the bakery a few times a week. Although it was much less frequent lately."

My eyebrows hiked. "Oh? She didn't need your help anymore?"

"I wouldn't say that..."

"Darling, there is no need to hold back with us," my mother sang. "We're all friends here."

Fighting the very strong urge to laugh, I kept my concentration in place and my face neutral. She was really selling it, and it was becoming comical. What kind of friends were they, really? The kind that met under false pretenses less than twenty-four hours ago? If I didn't need the man to talk, I'd tell him to run.

Instead of doing the decent thing, I only stared, playing the role of accessory to the crime perfectly.

William looked at me expectantly.

"What she said," I mumbled, shame warming my neck.

He cleared his throat and leaned into Mom's shoulder. In return, she squeezed his arm again, her smile slanting toward him. "I really shouldn't be saying anything," William said. "But the bakery wasn't exactly doing well these days. Financially."

My anticipation deflated. That wasn't exactly fresh information; Brandy had told me the same thing earlier. Maybe cornering the odd helper man wasn't the best idea. I watched my mother play with a ringlet of her hair flirtatiously. At least she was getting something out if it.

"You know, when that woman offered to buy the bakery, I told Reeba to go for it."

My ears perked up. "Which woman?"

"Pretty one across the street," he replied. His eyes darted to Mom guiltily, then drifted back to me. "The hotel owner. She came to Reeba weeks ago, promising a load of cash for the place. She mentioned expanding the hotel, I believe. I didn't quite catch it on account of being preoccupied otherwise."

Translation: he was eavesdropping and couldn't get any closer. I wet my lips and leaned on my elbows. "Isabella Beaumont was after Bakes and Cakes?"

When William nodded, my entire body froze. Was I right to think Isabella was involved in what happened to Mrs. Cevil? First Ridgewood, then the protection charm Harry found, and now this? Everything was pointing straight to the vampire. But why? What would Isabella want with a small town bakery? And why was she willing to kill for it?

I rolled the theory around in my head, shoving squares into circles to make it fit.

"Anyway," William said, interrupting my thoughts. "We had it out about the entire thing and Reeba told me to mind my own business. Which, in all fairness, I should have been doing. Said she'd call me when there was more work."

I scratched my head. "And did she?"

"Not a whisper," William said. "It was bizarre. Up until that point, she'd been an absolute pleasure to be around. Even asked to meet my mother when she was visiting next."

"Was that the last time you two spoke? The argument?"

He nodded slowly, his face scrunching as though he realized he had given too much away. "I'm sure she would have called eventually," he said in a hurry. "It's terrible what happened. I'm not sure what I'll do now."

For a brief moment, my mom and I exchanged quick glances, both of us thinking the same thing. The man was unbelievably selfish. Who thought about their own future when a woman was dead?

If there was anything real between Mom and William, I was certain it was over now.

On queue, Mom said, "Well, it is getting on, isn't it?" She pushed her chair back, retrieving her hand from William's arm, and nodded at the door. "Likely best we call it a night. Or day."

"Oh, of course," William agreed.

As my mother walked him to the front door to say goodbye, I jumped for my cellphone. My fingers moved quickly to dial Cilia's number in the hopes I would catch her before she finished her overnight shift. The phone rang and surprisingly, she picked it up on the first dial.

"Piper, hi," she said, her voice out of breath.

"Hi, Cilia," I said back. "I was wondering if I could speak with—" I paused, realizing something was amiss with my friend. "—Is everything all right? You sound winded."

A long exhale broke the silence on the line, followed by Cilia muttering under her breath. "Oh, it is definitely not all right. I've been running around like a chicken with her head cut off all morning. It's the Wild West over here!"

"Tourists?"

Cilia scoffed. "I wish. No, I'm afraid we have a bit of a situation on our hands, and everyone is knee deep in putting out fires."

"Anything I can help with?" I offered.

There was another sigh before Cilia said, "Not really. Not unless you have a locator spell I can use?"

"You must be desperate if you're asking me for magic help," I said, laughing. "What did you lose?"

Cilia was so quiet that, for a moment, I thought we lost the connection. When she spoke again, it was in a voice so soft, I could barely make it out. "Not what, who," my friend said. "Isabella never made it to her conference. She's been missing for days."

Well, this was not exactly how I thought things would go down. Mom and I had corralled an anxious Cilia to the bar down the street in the hopes of getting her mind off what happened with Isabella. Unfortunately, our plan backfired, and we now had a rambling, intoxicated witch on our hands.

And it wasn't even three o'clock yet.

"You don't think I know that she was awful?" Cilia asked. Her words slurred and there was a hiccup after every third one. "But she was on top of things. Honestly, ladies, the woman even had my bathroom breaks timed."

"Yikes," Mom said.

I kicked her boot under the table, catching a glimpse of the bartender, who was waving to get my attention. Thanking my lucky stars for the excuse to get away, I mumbled "be right back" and slipped out of the stuffy booth.

The Drunk Elephant, our local, and only bar, was surprisingly empty today. It was upsetting to say, but when it came to Orchard Hollow, there was no telling how wild people got on any given day. Since we had such an influx of vacationers on a regular basis, party mode was constantly engaged.

Today, though, there was not a soul in sight. Unless you counted the few regulars scattered through the dimly lit establishment, of course.

I walked briskly to the main bar situated against the rear wall of the large space, ignoring the stickiness causing my shoes to catch on the linoleum floor. The stained glass windows at my back cast a messy shadow of mixed colors on the white brick and made the bar resemble something out of a circus. The mismatched bottles stacked on the three long shelves stretching from side to side didn't help, especially since most of them appeared to be in need of replenishment. There was a picture of an elephant in a sombrero hanging between two shelves and a neon sign with the bar's name beneath it.

This place was a level of tacky even I didn't understand. I giggled, picturing Stella Rutherford here.

Not far from me, Cilia let out a loud sob and I cringed, speeding up to settle our tab so we could get her out and back home faster. At first, the idea of a couple of drinks to get my friend's mind off her boss's strange disappearance seemed like a great idea. It wasn't until Mom decided tequila shots were on the menu that things went south. Leave it to her to take the situation from bad to worse, then stiff me with the bill.

Not to mention the thing that had me wound up in knots for most of the day. If Isabella Beaumont was missing, she didn't kill Mrs. Cevil. But then why was she constantly popping up lately? And why did Mrs. Cevil have a protection charm against a vampire in her bakery?

"Another round?" the bartender, a young man I vaguely recognized from around town, asked.

I glanced over my shoulder in time to see Cilia pound a fist on the table. "I think we're all set," I replied. "Sorry about the table."

"No trouble at all," the young man said. "We get much worse around here. I haven't seen you by before. Are you visiting?"

I started to answer when another howl sounded

from our table. Smiling sheepishly, I patted the bar and said, "I should probably get her home."

"Understood. I'll get the bill for you."

Settling a very expensive tab, I thanked the young man and turned toward our table, ready to pour Cilia into a cab to get her home. As I spun around, I realized the women were surprisingly quiet. More importantly, they weren't alone.

Walking at a brisk pace, I made my way back to them.

"Piper! Glad to run into you," Ember said.

"Um, sure..."

What was she doing here in the afternoon? And who was watching the pharmacy? As far as I knew, the werewolf worked around the clock and never took a break. Plus, her kind weren't big on alcohol since the density of their blood made it near impossible to feel its effects. Then what was Ember doing at the Drunk Elephant, of all places?

I quirked a brow. "Is everything all right?"

"You could say that," the werewolf said. "I was surprised to see your mom back in town."

"Isn't she great?" Cilia asked, slurring her words.

Angling myself to shield Cilia from the werewolf, I nudged Mom to keep her distracted while I spoke to Ember. My friend needed to vent, but I didn't want her getting a reputation. Not that Ember was one to gossip, though these days, one could never be too sure who they spoke to around here.

Receiving the message loud and clear, Mom wrapped an arm around Cilia, said goodbye, and led the mumbling witch outside for some much needed fresh air. As soon as they left, I turned back to the werewolf. "Sorry about that. She's had a rough day."

"Trust me, if I could join her, I would."

I gulped. "Now I'm really worried," I said. "What's going on?"

"A few hiccups with the divorce," she said. "Nothing to worry about. I was actually looking for you about another matter."

"Oh?"

Ember tucked a loose strand from her bob behind her ears and nodded for me to get closer. I obeyed because no one wanted to piss off a werewolf, no matter how sweet they seemed. While I knew Ember would never harm a soul, I had no intention of seeing those teeth up close and personal.

When I was near enough not to be overheard, she whispered, "I looked more into what you came by about."

Ember wiggled her brows playfully and my ears perked up.

"What do you mean?"

Pointing to her nose, she brushed up against me to

get closer. Her face was so close to mine, our noses were inches away from touching. Adding more drama to the situation, Ember looked around the bar suspiciously. When she was satisfied no one cared about us — because there was literally no one here— she said, "I paid Bakes and Cakes a visit."

"The bakery?" I asked, baffled. "How did you get inside? And why?"

Ember waved me off as though I'd said the most ludicrous thing in the world. "Please, this town is not exactly built like a fortress. The door wasn't even locked." She shifted her weight, putting a sliver of space between our bodies. "I have to tell you, narrowing down scents in a public space is quite the task."

Steeling a trembling voice, I inhaled quickly.

"I don't understand. What scent were you looking for?"

The werewolf shrugged. "I'm not sure," she said. "At least I wasn't at first. I figured I could try to see if there was a smell I didn't recognize from around town, someone fresh. And it worked."

"No!" I smacked her arm.

"Yes," Ember whispered. "There was a peculiar smell that stood out against the rest. I followed it as best I could, but it tapered off around Third and Strongville Drive. I'm sorry I couldn't find the actual person, but I thought it might point you in a new direction." She coughed into her sleeve. "If you were still following up on this."

My head nodded furiously. "I am! I certainly am." Glancing at the door, I tried to tamp down my rising excitement as an idea pushed its way into my brain. I turned back to Ember. "You helped more than you know. Thank you!"

Telling her I'll repay the favor, I left the werewolf in the bar and rushed outside. My legs pumped as I barreled down the street toward Mom and Cilia who'd found a bench to sit on while they waited for me. Ignoring Cilia's nonsensical chatter, I briefly filled Mom in on what Ember told me.

"Why are you so excited about an intersection?" Mom asked.

"Hello? Third and Strongville! Doesn't that ring a bell?"

She shrugged, clueless. Exhaling, I pulled out my cellphone and checked online for a number, then dialed it. The line rang three times before someone picked up. A bubbly, high-pitched voice sang out on the other end. "Nolan's Bed and Breakfast, how can I help you?"

"Miss Nolan!" I exclaimed cheerfully. "Piper Addison here. How are you?"

"Oh, Piper. Good, good. How are things at the cafe?"

It had been a while since I visited the owner of the local bed and breakfast, though she and Gran were on great terms. Before Gran died, Miss Nolan would often come to visit us in the farmhouse and she was a pleasure to be around. She reminded me a lot of Gran, minus the witch part. I kept telling myself that I needed to drop in on her more often, but time usually got away from me. Now that I had her on the phone, guilt ate away at me because of my reason for calling. Instead of checking in, I was about to trick her into giving me information on her guests.

Convincing myself it was for the greater good, I made a note to stop by later with some goodies from the cafe.

"Piper?"

I shook my head. "Still here," I said, quickly. "Funny you mentioned the cafe. I am in a bit of a spot."

"Oh? Anything I can help with?"

"As a matter of fact, you can," I told her. "Do you have someone staying with you at the moment?"

There was a scuffle on the line before Miss Nolan said, "Why yes, I do. Haven't had a tenant in weeks until now," she explained. "It's been winding down with the season changing."

"Of course," I agreed. "Well, this is a bit odd, but perhaps you can help. A customer is friends with your tenant, it seems. They wanted to send over a little surprise from the cafe, a carafe of coffee, some baked goods, that sort of thing. The thing is, Rory took the order and I cannot for the life of me make out her handwriting. It says Nolan's Bed and Breakfast clear as day, but the person's name is illegible."

Beside me, Mom's eyebrows hiked and her jaw unhinged as she listened to me spew lie after lie at the poor woman. Even Cilia stopped yammering to hear what was going on.

My cheeks burned; I turned away to keep from breaking character. "I'd ask Rory," I added, "but she's gone for the day and you know, teenagers. She'll never pick up her phone when you need her to."

"Don't I know it," Miss Nolan said, chuckling. "I remember those days with my daughters."

"Any chance you can give me the name so I can get it right on the card?" I asked. On the other line, Miss Nolan rattled off the tenant's name eagerly, clearly excited to be in on the action. I smiled, turning around to face Mom and Cilia. "Linna Cruller. Got it. Thank you so much! I'll make a separate basket for you too for the trouble."

Getting off the phone, I looked at my mother. My mouth opened, then closed as I took in her panicked expression. Putting the phone away, I raked my fingers through my hair, asking, "What's wrong?"

Mom ran her tongue over her front teeth.

"Linna Cruller is a Sister," she said. "She's part of the coven."

CHAPTER 18

"No, no, no!" I ducked out of the way as a rogue croissant flew across the room. The doughy oval smashed into the mantel, crumbling to pieces before falling to the floor. A few bits fell into the fireplace and the stench of burned bread filled the living room.

I smacked my forehead. "How was that?"

Watching from the kitchen with wide eyes and a shocked expression, my mom lowered her arms and shook her head.

"I believe I speak for all of us when I say more practice is needed," Stella Rutherford said from her hiding spot on the stairs.

Groaning, I lowered to perch on the edge of the

red armchair across from the couch. "Stella is right, I'm not getting any closer to having a handle on this."

Taking three long strides, my mother crossed the space between us. For a moment, I thought she was going to hug me but she kept walking until she reached the fireplace. She bent down to pick up a piece of the croissant and tossed it into her mouth with a smile. "Patience, honey," she uttered between loud chews. "Defensive magic takes years to master and you're trying to tackle it in a matter of hours. You'll get there."

"Before or after Linna kills me?"

Chuckling, Stella swooped in between us, her ghostly body almost entirely clear. She clapped her hands together in mock cheerfulness. "Besties for all eternity! Fun!"

I took off a slipper and flung it toward her corporeal self-absorbed head. The ghost hissed, swerving out of the way in time to avoid the hit. Unfortunately, my mother was not as lucky and the slipper smacked her thigh before falling lamely to rest beside a scorched croissant flake.

"Ladies, please, have some decorum," she scolded as she wiped her jeans clean. "We are on a tight deadline to get Piper ready for what is coming and we could do without the bickering." She looked down at the bread bits on the carpet and added, "Clearly, we have our work cut out for us."

No kidding. I wasn't sure why Mom thought she could help me master witch magic when it was clear I may never have had it to begin with. If anything, we should have been working on my super creepy underworld powers, but when I suggested it, her face paled and she changed the subject. Even after being here for almost a week, Mom was tight-lipped about the entire thing.

Not to mention my father.

My eyes narrowed on her slender frame, swallowed by layers of silk and chiffon in a rainbow of colors. What was she hiding from me? And why?

By now, I was convinced Gran knew about my wonky magic and who my father was and she went to her grave with the information. Mom was my only chance to find out, and she refused to talk. If frustration had a face, it would be wearing mine. How was I supposed to help stop the Sisters of the River and protect myself in the process if no one spoke to me about anything of value? I was a forty-plus-year-old woman who was being treated like a child and it irked me to no small extent.

"Instead of wasting time barbequing baked goods," Stella said with a smirk, "why don't you nip the problem at the root?"

Peeling my eyes away from my mother, I turned to the ghost, my body crooked. "What do you mean?"

"You know there's a Sister in town..."

"And?"

Stella's features darkened as she spun in a circle, her arms stretched to the side. The long ponytail she wore passed through a vase and I cringed, momentarily forgetting she can't knock it over. "What better way to greet a fellow witch than to invite her over for a cup of tea?"

"Stella, that is the most dangerous thing—"

"What did she say?" Mom asked.

I grimaced. "She said to ask Linna to come over. Apparently, dying is her best idea."

"Hmm," Mom mumbled under her breath. "Your familiar might be onto something here. I could ask Linna over under the pretense of introducing you and we can question her to see how much she knows. And how much the other Sisters know."

The line between my lips stretched out as my mood soured further. This couldn't be happening. "Are you two feeling all right?" I asked. "You want to invite the very witch we're trying to protect the world against into our home? By choice? For... what was it? A cup of tea?"

"A glass of whiskey would be preferable if I recall

Linna correctly," Mom said. "But yes, I think it's a wonderful idea. Great thinking Stella!"

My familiar tipped an imaginary hat in Mom's direction.

Honestly, it was bad enough that I usually felt like I was on the outside of Stella and Harry Houdini's interactions, but now I had to put up with it from Mom too. Whatever the two reckless women had in mind— I was on board with it. And yet... Bringing Linna here would save me a lot of trouble of having to track her down and keep an eye on her whereabouts. And the farmhouse wasn't without its safety features.

I shot a glare at the runes covering the frame of the front door. If Linna had any ill will towards me, those babies would blast her butt with enough magic to knock out an elephant.

My frown flipped around.

"So, what do you say honey?" Mom asked.

I looked from her to Stella, then back again. "You get the protection charms, I'll get the whiskey."

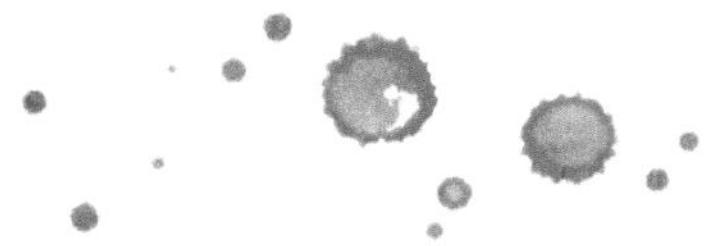

Linna Cruller was not who I expected at all. The witch trembled in the living room armchair, her long fingers crushing the whiskey glass in her hands. Eyes darting nervously around the room, she struck me as someone who had very little confidence, the opposite of what I imagined a member of the world's oldest coven to be. Her demeanor didn't scream, "I can end you for looking at me funny." No, Linna had more of a squirrel searching for a nut appearance and not that of a murderer.

And yet Mrs. Cevil, the woman working in secret to bring down the coven, was dead and Linna was in town. It didn't look good on paper.

"So, Linna," my mom said to break the awkward silence. "What brings you to Orchard Hollow? I hadn't seen in you in what? Two years? Three?"

"Five," the witch answered.

Mom cleared her throat uncomfortably. "Right. Back in—"

"Ridgewood," Linna answered matter-of-factly. She brought the whiskey glass to her lips, smelled it, then put it back down in her lap.

There was that name again. What was it about Ridgewood that made it such a popular spot? As far as I knew, it wasn't anything special and yet I kept hearing the name come up over and over again.

I put a pin in the thought, shifting my weight around so I sat more comfortably next to Mom.

"You two look a lot alike," Linna said. Her dark

eyes rolled over me and she pulled on one of the many tiny braids hanging loose around her neckline as she spoke. For the first time since she came by, I noticed the lines creasing around her eyes and on her brow, her age showing through an otherwise flawless facade. "I didn't realize you had children."

Beside me, Mom bristled. "Just the one."

I was seriously beginning to regret agreeing to this plan. Not only did Mom and Linna appear to be complete strangers, but I wasn't getting a stabby-stabby killer vibe off the witch. The hunt for the person responsible for Mrs. Cevil's murder was taking its toll, and all I wanted was to take a hot bath and to crawl into bed. Instead, I had to sit in between two Sisters— one fake, one real— and watch them make small talk.

It was exhausting.

"This is about as fun as watching my dear old Arthur do the taxes," Stella whispered in my ear over my shoulder. "I never thought I'd say this, but I'm going to go find the rodent to see what he's up to. Holler if you're about to bite the bullet."

My hair whooshed over my face as the ghost vanished from sight. Noticing the motion, Linna's eyes flared, but she didn't say anything. Her gaze continued to shift around the farmhouse like she was memorizing its blueprints.

To break in later, perhaps?

I shivered, the thought of the witch sneaking into my home made shivers trip down my spine. Raising my empty wineglass, I asked, "Anyone up for a refill?"

"I'm good for now," Linna said.

Shockingly, Mom agreed with her. Staying in my spot, I was itching in the confines of my skin and begging for time to move at a faster clip. What a colossal waste the evening was proving to be.

"So, Linna," Mom said, jarring me back to the room. "Are you in town on Sister business?"

Wow. Straight to the point. I swallowed the excess saliva threatening to drown me and peeled my eyes off Mom to look at Linna.

The witch was as caught off guard as I was, it seemed. "I beg your pardon?" she asked, staring daggers into Mom.

"No need to be coy," Mom said, waving her hand dismissively. "Piper here knows all about our activities. You don't expect me to keep my daughter in the dark, do you? Not when she is next in line for a spot in the coven."

My head spun a three sixty. *A spot in the what now?* Drawing little attention to herself, Mom pinched my leg when Linna wasn't paying attention. Of course, she was putting on another show.

"Not official business, no," the witch replied coyly.

A sly grin tugged at the corners of my mother's lips

as she crossed her long legs and leaned closer to Linna. "You're being quite vague, my dear," she told the witch. "I'm beginning to think you might be keeping secrets from me. Sisters share all, don't we?"

Okay, Mom. Take it down a notch. There's no way she's going to—

"You got me!" Linna said, interrupting my disbelief. Her arms shot up in surrender and she chuckled, her voice dry. "I was visiting a friend from back in the day. But it was a surprise."

Mom's brow twitched. "Ah. A little romantic spying... Do tell."

"I wouldn't say romantic..."

A nod of Mom's head made the witch's cheeks burn a bright red. The color spread down her neck and she pulled up her cashmere turtleneck to cover her embarrassment. "All right, fine. There's a man I knew when I was younger. One of the Sisters mentioned he'd be in town this week and I figured a rendezvous was in order."

"How fun!" Mom exclaimed, her hands clapped together.

Before us, Linna slumped her shoulders, her small body disappearing further into the cushions of the armchair. "Not exactly," she said with a sigh. "He's seeing someone else. Turns out that's why he was in Orchard Hollow in the first place."

"I'm sorry to hear that," I offered. "I completely understand how you feel."

"Oh, yes! Piper here has had her share of bad luck when it comes to men," Mom added. "Haven't you, honey?"

I scoffed. Said the woman who quite literally erased the father of her only child from our lives. My teeth knocked together, and I started to stand up, suddenly wishing to drown the night away in a second glass of wine. Maybe even a third. As I walked to the kitchen, I overheard Mom ask Linna more about the mystery man she chased all the way into our small town.

"We've known each other since we were kids," Linna said. "But then you know how it goes. Life got in the way and the coven, well, the coven needed me. I went my way and Tom went his."

The name made me pause. I turned slowly, my fingers white-knuckling the glass. Gaze catching Mom's, I watched her offer a tiny nod of recognition, telling me we were on the same page. How many Toms were visiting Orchard Hollow because of a woman? Only one that I knew of.

I put the glass on the bar counter before I shattered it. "Does Tom have a last name?" I asked.

"Sorrelis," Linna answered. "Do you two know each other?"

Shaking my head, I proceeded to walk back to the kitchen to gather my thoughts. Another string on the hypothetical crime board was stretching into place. How was Tom Sorrelis connected to so many witches in our town? It couldn't be a coincidence that he knew Linna when they were younger or that Mrs. Cevil was his client. Not to mention dating Isabella. The man was in the center of this entire web; I knew it. The problem was that I couldn't prove it.

Unless...

Wine spilled down the side of the glass and I stopped pouring, narrowly avoiding making a huge mess.

Isabella's face flashed before my eyes, a new plan forming. If I could find the vampire, I had a chance to answer some of the questions I had about Tom Sorrelis. I looked into the living room solemnly. Perhaps before another witch lost her life.

CHAPTER 19

My finger wrapped an incoherent beat against the window as I watched the empty driveway. Upstairs, Mom sang off tune, the shower running at full blast. She woke up extra giddy this morning, yet I knew without a doubt that seeing Linna shook her. We had a Sister in our house. Mom left us for years because of some convoluted plan to protect me from the very person who sat on the couch Gran reupholstered with her own hands.

And it was all for nothing.

The Sisters now knew where we lived, where *I* lived, and we didn't get anything out of it. Linna wasn't a cold-blooded murderer set on destroying Mrs. Cevil because she found out she wanted the Sisters gone. She was a lustful woman, following a sleazy man.

I really should have known better. If Linna was here to take care of the witches plotting against the coven, Mom would have suffered the same fate as Mrs. Cevil. But the Sister was genuinely surprised to see her in town. She was even more surprised to find out about me. A fact I hated had come to light.

There was no telling what the coven might think about Mom hiding her only child. Especially since she'd now put me joining their stupid coven on the table.

I still had no idea why she'd said that. It was likely the first thing that popped into her head so as not to blow her cover. Unfortunately, it put me right in the middle of her twisted game of cat and mouse. My breath came out short. I hadn't realized until that very moment that I hadn't doubted Mom's motive once in the last few days.

That was probably a huge mistake.

A loud vibration pierced the silence of the farm-house, making me jump. I spun around to see my phone dance across the mantel where I left it, an inch away from meeting its doom and tumbling off the edge. Diving for it, I caught it in time before it fell. My chest heaved; evidence of my poor physical abilities coming to light.

Brow furrowed, I checked the screen and picked up. "Joe?" I asked. My eyes floated to the clock on the kitchen wall, the time of day surprising me. "It's not even seven. Is everything all right?"

"Morning, Piper. Sorry to call so early, but it seems to be the only free time I have for the rest of the day." He breathed in deeply on the other end and I could almost smell his peppermint scent through the phone. "I thought I'd check to see how things went with Ember before the day gets away from me."

I paced the length of the living room as I desperately tried to formulate a concise summary of the last few days. There was no short way to tell Joe everything that had happened and the explanation held even less appeal, considering how little I'd been able to uncover. The murder of Mrs. Cevil was a mystery I couldn't solve, and it had become an itch I couldn't help but scratch. Above my head, an object fell on the floor and my mom cursed violently after it.

At least I wasn't alone in this.

I stopped walking and looked out the bay window, surprised when I saw the first glimpse of light snow drifting down. "She was shockingly helpful without even using her abilities," I told Joe. "I've hit a dead end, though. Again. And there were a few other hiccups that happened, but it's probably best to leave that story for when I see you again. When do you think you'll be heading back?"

"I'm aiming for the end of the week," Joe answered. My childish heart pitter pattered in my chest. "And I have a surprise when I return."

My mouth parted to answer, then closed. A glimmer of light reflecting off a shiny surface caught my attention. I pursed my lips to expel a breath, walking toward the armchair in the living room. Bending down to sit on my knees, I bent forward to see what it was that I saw. Something was wedged between the seat and the back of the chair, a silvery material I knew didn't belong in the farmhouse.

I reached my hand in to yank it out and brought it to my face with a gasp.

"Piper?"

Dragging my attention to the phone, I cleared my throat, my fingers tightly wrapped around the object I'd discovered. "Sorry, Joe, I'll need to call you back later."

He started to ask for details, but I quickly said goodbye and hung up. As much as I wanted to stay on the phone with him, I couldn't. My chest tightened and my leg muscles ached as I balanced in a half-crouch.

Turning my hand around, I inspected the small silver pouch, bringing it up to my nose. The smell was so familiar, I nearly toppled backwards. "What are you doing here?"

I stood up and walked to the staircase, eyes traveling up to the second floor.

"Did you leave a vampire protection charm in the living room?" I yelled out.

"Huh?" Mom shouted back over the sound of the shower.

I shook my head. "Never mind!"

Pacing again, I covered the entire ground floor, the charm dangling from my sweaty fingers. Mom never mentioned vampires before. Why would she bother leaving a charm against one here, of all places? Considering that I never told her about the charm Harry found or that I suspected Isabella was somehow involved in the baker's death, she would have no reason to plant one in our home. If she wanted to protect us from a vampire, she'd have told me about it.

Besides, Mom was terrible at charm making; that was Gran's specialty.

I glanced at the pouch, eyes traveling between it and the armchair. There was only one other witch that graced the farmhouse in the last little while, and she sat in that same chair.

But why would Linna leave this behind? Why hide it?

My gaze flicked up the stairs as I pocketed the

charm and walked to the front door. Grabbing my car keys and coat, I called out, "Be right back!" and slammed the door behind me. Thanks to Mom, I knew where Linna was staying and Miss Nolan's Bed and Breakfast was only a ten-minute drive away. If I hurried, I could catch her before she left for the day.

Not bothering to lock up, I ran down the driveway, buttoning my coat as I made the brisk way to the car. The engine rattled before turning on and I thanked the stars when the heat turned on full blast. One of these days, I would need to take my baby in to the mechanic. For now, the Russian roulette of turning on the ignition would have to do.

Stepping on the gas, I made my way past the copse of trees lining the property and toward the cliff-side road that led into town. My eyes stayed glued on the road, occasionally checking the rear-view when I remembered that I was almost run off this same road recently by Stella's killer. You'd think after that I'd avoid taking the scenic route, but it was usually quicker and what were the chances of the same thing happening twice?

Since I was nowhere near getting to the bottom of the crime now, I was pretty certain I wasn't on a killer's hit list.

One could never be too safe.

I looked behind me again— coast clear.

Being busy with make-believe stalkers, I almost didn't notice the flashing lights along the coastline. I pulled my foot off the gas to slow down and inspected the beach. There had to be at least five cars down there, three of which had the familiar paint of the Orchard Hollow police department. I also spotted an ambulance and a fire truck alongside rolls of yellow tape that sectioned off a portion of the sand.

"What is going down there?"

To my right, the road turned off to give people a chance to exit. I gauged the time I had left and grimaced. What to do? Any other person would have kept driving, but not me. I did the exact opposite. Veering the Beetle off the main road, I took the off-beaten path leading to the beach. By the time I parked in the parking lot, a small crowd had already started to gather around the scene. I noticed a few uniformed officers walking back and forth to keep the nosy bystanders at bay.

As I approached, one of the officers made a beeline straight for me with his hand outstretched.

"No entrance," he said, his tone harsh and unwavering.

I took a step back instantly. "What happened here?"

"I'm not at liberty to say," the officer answered. "I suggest you—"

"It's quite all right, Sloan," another man interrupted. From behind the first man's shoulders, a wide-brimmed hat appeared, and my body relaxed at the sight of the sheriff. "You can let her through. She's with me."

Romero lifted the yellow crime scene tape, and I ducked underneath, slipping to the other side. Whispers rose behind us as I followed the sheriff down the beach and away from the parking lot.

We walked in silence. I matched his steps beat by beat. Now that I was down here, I could see more clearly why there was a need for all the cars and tape. Something happened on the beach. Something terrible. I spotted another knowing face not far from us and my stomach dropped into my boots.

"Why is the coroner here?" I asked.

Romero's eyes flared, his expression fermenting. "I'm sure you can guess at the answer to that question," he said. "I'm glad you're here, Miss Addison. Saves me the trouble of calling you into the station later."

Uh-oh. That did not sound good. I swallowed the lump in my throat to clear it and looked around. Past where I saw the coroner— a man in a suit on the beach is hard to miss— lay a body bag. My eyes watered, the horror of the situation dawning on me as it carved its way up my body.

I forced myself to look away from the scene. "What happened? Who is that?"

The sheriff cleared his throat but didn't speak.

"Sheriff?"

"There's not an easy way to say this," he uttered. "A tourist discovered the body of a woman on their morning jog. It appears she drowned and the tide must have carried her to shore."

My body stilled, thoughts racing in my mind as I worked to make sense of his words.

"Why would you need me at the station, sheriff?" I asked, afraid I already knew the answer.

For a moment, Romero appeared shaken. I had never seen the man act anything but put together so his inability to express his thoughts, when he usually had no problem speaking his mind, was unnerving. He rubbed the back of his neck until his skin turned a bright shade of red. "Because you were the last person to see the victim," he finally said. "At least according to my sources."

I didn't need him to say any more; I already knew whose lifeless body lay under the black tarp in the middle of the beach. My fingers curled into a fist around the charm bag in my pocket as I said, "It's Linna Cruller, isn't it?" I asked.

Romero nodded briefly, confirming my suspicion. My chest constricted, and I found it hard to stand still.

I swayed from side to side, my gaze swinging like a pendulum.

"I have some questions about your meeting last night. Best to get it over with," the sheriff said.

I barely heard him. My eyes locked on the body bag or, more pointedly, on the sand around it. I brushed past the sheriff, ignoring his calls for me as I marched toward Linna. Ducking down, I placed my palm on the ground and shivered.

"Ma'am, you can't be near—"

I blocked out the rest of what the young officer said. Instead, I rose to stand and walked around Linna in a tight circle. My gaze never left the sand. Footsteps followed behind me, the sheriff wondering what I was up to. Surprisingly, he stayed quiet and let me think.

Taking another round, I scrunched my brow and rubbed my temples. The sand surrounding Linna's body was disturbed, which was no shock considering how many people had been in the area. There were so many footsteps and patterns that anyone else would have missed it; I almost did as well. Except that now that I was here, I couldn't see anything else. Under all the imprints left from hurried feet and the drag marks from carrying her out of the water, you could see the faint impressions of etchings that didn't belong here.

What the sheriff and his team missed in the midst of all their investigating was that Linna's body didn't simply wash up on the shore. It washed up to lay in the dead center of a rune circle, one that had been scrubbed away.

My eyes widened until I could feel pressure from behind my temples. Linna Cruller didn't drown.

This had magic written all over it.

CHAPTER 20

"This is the last time I bail you out of jail."

I let out a long sigh at my mother's back as we climbed out of the cab, my eyes rolling dramatically. "You have literally never had to bail me out," I corrected her. "And all you did was pick me up because the Beetle wouldn't start and I left my wallet at home."

Mom huffed and puffed as she climbed the porch steps. Her long silk skirt flowed behind her and the bottom lace got caught under her cowboy boots with each step. When we walked in, she removed her faux-fur coat and exposed a sequin corset cut so low I could almost see her belly button.

I shuddered. "Isn't that a little too much for a weekday?" *Or ever?*

"Do you like it?" Mom asked. "I found it in one of your grandmother's boxes in the attic. It's French."

The thought of Gran in the shiny monstrosity was horrifying, and I had to tuck it away into the dark crevices of my brain to never see the light of day again. My eye twitched as Mom did a double spin, the silk of the skirt slicing against my shins. I cringed visibly. "How are you in a good mood right now?"

"Why? Because of Linna?" She shrugged. "Look, I'm sorry she's gone, and it's a shame how it happened, but this is a Sister we're talking about here. We're all better off, trust me."

I reared back, the coat rack hitting between my shoulders. Was I hearing correctly? When did my mother, the woman who loved everyone a little too much, become so cynical and cruel? Sure, if they were up to what Mom said, the Sisters of the River had to be stopped, but at what cost? I wasn't about to wipe out an entire coven of women and I certainly wasn't relieved one of them ended up dead on our shorelines. Unlike my mother, who was quite literally dancing for joy.

I eyed her harrowingly. "It's still wrong."

"Of course, honey," she whispered. "Murder is very wrong. But so is trying to end the entire freaking world. I'm not saying I'm glad Linna's gone. All I'm saying is it's one less dark magic witch to worry about."

I failed to see the difference.

"Besides," Mom continued, "the runes you saw only further my point. I bet you any money that whoever killed Linna got to Reeba as well."

"But why? Linna was a sister. If the coven was getting rid of people working against them, why take one of their own?"

Brow furrowing, Mom finally took off her ridiculous coat and walked to the kitchen. She filled a kettle and turned on the stove, her eyes scanning the kitchen for the tea selection.

"Top right drawer," I instructed.

She nodded, sliding across the floor in one fluid motion. "I'm not sure why, but I know a Sister did this." Plopping a tea bag into a mug, she sniffed the air and sighed in satisfaction. "I'm going to tell you a secret, but I don't want you to freak out."

I was freaking out before she even finished the sentence. Mom must have sensed my agitation because she said, "I mean it, Piper. Wipe that face off or I won't share."

Disguising my annoyance with a forced smile, I performed an exaggerated bow and ended it with a twirl of my hand.

"Cute," Mom said, chuckling. "As I was saying, I

may or may not have done something to get the attention of the coven a few nights ago."

My knees locked up. "What did you do?"

"Nothing too out there," she admitted. "Only a
little dark magic that would leave a trace. I tried to
summon Malachi from a picture. Never mind that. I
figured if a Sister was in town, it might draw them out
into the open. But now..."

"Yes?"

Mom's gaze dropped to the floor, her skin blanching. "What if all I did was put a target on Linna's
back? Whoever hurt Reeba would have sensed the
spell, and it may have led them to Linna instead of me.
No one in the coven knows I'm from Orchard Hollow.
I made sure there was no trace to bring them back
here."

Alert bells went off in my head as I listened to her
speak. On the one hand, it was a relief to know Mom
wasn't practicing dark magic for the reason I thought
she was. On the other, she'd lied to me about it and
now a witch may have paid the price for her careless-
ness. And why bother using dark magic to summon my
father? She could have just called him. I scratched my
chin, thoughts wandering. "Why would Linna practicing dark magic make her a target for the coven? Isn't
that their main slogan?" I asked.

"The Sisters don't practice solitary spells," Mom

replied. "They don't even trust their own members. If whoever killed Reeba thought a Sister was using dark magic alone, they may have suspected foul play."

"You're suggesting a Sister took Linna's life because she thought the witch and Mrs. Cevil were in cahoots?"

Mom nodded slowly. "A case of mistaken identity."

"They targeted Linna in your place..." I whispered. The more I thought about it, the more it made sense. Mom may have been on the right track. Maybe working with her wasn't the worst idea; she did know the coven inside and out and I had to admit, Linna's death was no doubt of the magical variety. My hand reached into a pocket to pull out the charm. I might as well lay all my cards on the table. "I think this may be Linna's work."

Mom crossed the distance between us in one long stride and snatched the charm from my hands. "You found it here?"

"Yes," I answered. "And Harry Houdini found a similar one at the bakery."

"The raccoon?"

I laughed. "He's very resourceful. Anyway, I was on my way to ask Linna about it but then... Well, you know." My head throbbed as I recalled the body bag on the beach. I shook off the thought, keeping myself grounded in the present. "It can't be a coincidence. Both victims had vampire protection charms; it has to be related."

"Isn't there a vampire that went missing recently?"

She was finally keeping up. It was reassuring to know that Mom came to the same conclusion about Isabella as me. Maybe I wasn't pulling at imaginary strings after all. I took the charm back from her and inspected the rune stitched into the silver bag. "It is unlikely timing that Isabella Beaumont is nowhere to be found. As far as I know, she is usually very accountable."

"Beaumont..." Mom said under her breath. "The name sounds so familiar. Is it French?"

What is with this woman and France? My mouth opened to speak, but a yawn escaped. I rubbed my eyes, exhaustion suddenly taking over me. The morning did a number on my energy level and for a moment, I sympathized with the warlocks in our town. A few chaotic hours exhausted me. I could only imagine how awful it must have been to feel this way after every time I used magic.

A memory of Tom Sorrelis ran through my mind. Did he appear to be tired when I spoke to him? A spell dark enough to kill would certainly weaken a warlock and he didn't seem all that out of it. Cocky, yes. Tired, not as much. Besides, what reason would

Tom have to hurt a childhood friend who was in love with him?

"Honey?"

I pressed on my hot and blurry eyes. "Will you be all right on your own for a while?" I asked. "I think I could use a lie down."

Getting back to her tea, Mom waved me off, and I took the chance to escape upstairs for some desperately needed rest. As soon as I neared the bed, my body curled in on itself and I fell into the fluffy blanket with a satisfied moan. One quick power nap and I'd be back on my feet. I knew it.

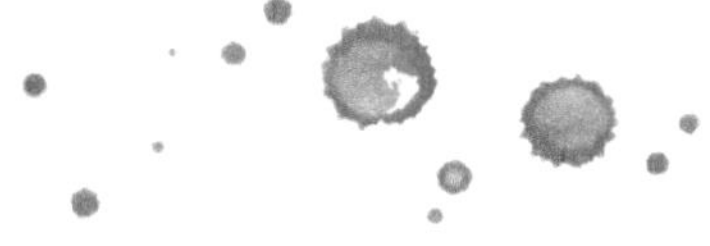

I awoke to the sound of screaming. Around me, the room was filled with smoke and my paper-thin lungs burned as I gasped for air. I coughed, my chest seizing from the added stress. Dry eyes blinking rapidly, I glanced out the window, shocked by how dark it was.

How long was I asleep?

It didn't matter. As soon as the brain fog of sleep cleared, panic took over. The farmhouse smelled like a firepit and my room was quickly filling up with gray smoke.

I jumped up in bed, eyes flicking to the closed door. Beneath it, smoke continued to pile into the room, and I had to cover my mouth and nose with my arm to keep from breathing it in. The screaming I'd heard before started again, my name being called over and over again.

"Mom!" I shouted as I hopped off the bed and headed for the door.

My hand wrapped over the handle and I yelped, yanking my hand away from the heat. Sweat beaded on my forehead, my body shivering. I whipped my head around the room, my body frozen with fear. "Mom! What's happening?"

"The house is on fire!"

No kidding. I tried the handle again and shrieked. It was even hotter now.

"Use your shirt sleeve," a voice said from behind me.

I spun around to face Stella. "What's going on down there?" I asked the ghost. "What fire?"

"No time to explain," my familiar said. "You need to move it, and fast. Use your shirt to open the door. Most of the flames are contained to the rear of the house, so you should be fine to get out."

Not bothering to argue, I followed her instructions and pulled down my shirt sleeve. When I gripped the handle, the heat I felt before had lessened and I was able to twist it and yank the door hard enough to open. A cloud of smoke hit my face, and I teetered backward, covering my mouth to keep from suffocating. A flashing red spark landed on my shirt, singeing the material instantly.

"Shoot!" I yelped.

"That shirt is ugly anyway," Stella snipped. "Get going!"

I stopped to wait for her, then hurried out. Stella couldn't get any deader and I had no intention of joining her in the ghost realm. My feet pounded the hardwood as I raced down the stairs, jumping the final two to land at the bottom. At my back, the flames Stella mentioned rose high into the air, growing larger by the second. They licked at my skin as I ran to put distance between myself and the danger. I squinted to make out the damage, but it was impossible to see through all the smoke.

My head swivelled to the front door and relief flooded my body when I saw Mom standing there. She was wearing her fleece pajamas, so I gathered she must have also dozed off only to wake up to the disaster we now faced.

She waved me over, and I dashed across the room, getting to her as quickly as my body would take me.

"What the heck is going on?" I asked when I reached her.

Gripping my arm, she pulled us both outside, where Stella already stood waiting. "Do you remember the rain summoning I taught you when you were little?" Mom asked.

"Vaguely," I admitted. Out of the corner of my eye, I saw the side of the house go up in flames and a shudder ran down my spine. "I'll give it another go."

Mom reached for my hand and gave it a quick squeeze, then dropped on all fours. Using her index finger, she drew a circle around us on the earth and slashed a few water runes at the five points. Her body moved quickly, so fast I barely registered what she was doing until it was too late.

One second my mom was crouching on the ground beside me and the next she had her palm sliced open and was slapping an imprint of her bloody hand onto the dirt.

"Mom! What are you doing?"

She looked up at me and winked. "Giving it a little oomph," she said. "The Sisters weren't entirely useless in the time I spent with them."

"Now that's magic I can get behind," Stella said.

I deadpanned the ghost, waiting until Mom was standing again to take her hand. She took the lead, her lips moving fast as she recited the spell to call on a storm. I listened carefully, memorizing the words before joining her. Together, we spoke faster and louder, our words intertwining. Around us, the energy of our magic swirled in circles, gusts of wind pouring out of our bodies and into the air.

I looked up as the first drop of water hit my forehead. It was working.

A tug on my sleeve jarred me back, and I continued to say the summoning words until the rain intensified. It took several repetitions, but we finally did it. The sky above us thundered angrily, clouds gathering over our heads. Rain pelted my skin, and I turned to my mother, amazed by the look of concentration on her face. I could watch Mom work magic forever. Her entire being encompassed it and it was in moments like this that I remembered how strong of a witch she was. No wonder the paranormals in town flocked to her.

"It worked," Mom said finally.

I followed her gaze to the house, my heart shattering. While it was true that the rain helped extinguish the fires, removing it completely, the damage had already been done. The entire side of the farmhouse was charred from the flames and the pieces of siding that hadn't fallen off were hanging on for dear life. It would take time to repair the damage, not to mention cost an arm and a leg.

I better find a way to draw more customers into Bean Me Up and fast.

A flash of movement near the trees caught my attention. I pulled away from Mom, stepping over the circle to get a better vantage point. For the briefest of moments, I swore I saw Isabella Beaumont standing between two large oaks.

"What is it, honey?"

I rubbed my eyes with the back of my palms. "Nothing. My mind is playing tricks on me," I answered. "We should see about cleaning all this up."

"I'll work on adding protection runes."

Pausing, I looked at my mother. "Why?"

"Isn't it obvious?" she asked. "The fire wasn't an accident. Someone is sending a message and I think we both know who."

"The Sisters."

Mom's eyes narrowed. "Might be a good idea to call the sheriff. Maybe get a patrol car to come around every so often."

"Absolutely not!" I said, my hand raised. "You are definitely right. This is paranormal business, but that's all the more reason not to call. I can't put any more lives in danger for my own protection. Especially not human lives. If the Sisters came after us, we have to handle it ourselves."

Mom scoffed, but turned around to walk back into the house. When she reached the front door, she turned halfway, her eyes piercing into me. "Whatever you're planning, you'd better do it fast," she said. "The fire was a message. We're next."

The bones left my legs, turning them into jelly. I wrapped my arms around my waist, scanning the trees once more. Nothing but darkness stared back at me. Mom was right. We were sent a very clear message tonight. Whoever did it knew where we lived and from the looks of the damage to the house, they were powerful. If I wished to go up against them, I needed help.

The Sisters may be strong witches but I bet they didn't have a warlock they could call on; especially not one that might have a personal vendetta against the ones who killed his childhood friend.

The woodsy smell of the Rose Hollow Hotel enveloped me. I stood with my knuckles hovering an inch away from the door, trying to work up the courage to knock. After the incident at the farmhouse, Mom agreed to stay behind in case whoever set the fire returned while I made my way into town. Now that I was here, I wished we had traded places. The last thing I wanted to do was beg Tom, the sleazeball warlock, for help.

And yet here I was, standing in front of his hotel room door.

Biting the inside of my cheek, I raised my hand and rapped on the door, my stomach pitched violently with anticipation. I wasn't sure why I was so wary of coming here; what was the worst the warlock could do? Send me on my way? If that happened, I'd be back to square one, but I'd figure something out. As Stella said, I was resourceful when I needed to be. Her description involved comparing me to a Cocker Spaniel, but I chose not to dwell on that part.

A hard object hit the wood floor and rolled on the other side of the door. I froze, my knees knocking. Slowly, the door slid open, and Tom Sorrelis appeared in the gap.

I breathed out a relieved breath when I saw he was fully dressed and we weren't in danger of a robe incident this time.

"You again," the warlock said.

Tonight, he lacked the purring drawl he had before when he refused to stop flirting with me. Instead, Tom's demeanor was that of a broken man. His hair was mussed, strands sticking out in every direction. There were dark bags under his eyes and he smelled distinctly of hard alcohol.

I held onto the doorframe as Tom's red eyes draped over me.

"Yes, hello," I coughed out. "Sorry to bother you so late. I hope I'm not interrupting."

Tom raised an empty whiskey glass. "I was about to pour another," he said.

It took me a moment to realize that was an invitation for me to come in. As the warlock stepped aside to make room for me to pass, I glanced over my shoulder at the camera mounted in the hallway and wondered if Cilia was watching. Probably not; my friend had her work cut out for her with her boss missing. It turned out running a hotel in a small town a month before holiday season was not an easy task.

I hoped for Cilia's sake that she'd be free of the added workload soon. My heart pounded in my ears. She may not be so lucky if it turned out I was right and Isabella had a hand in the two murders. The vampire may well be on the run right now.

The door closed behind me. Tom brushed past, heading straight for the minibar. My gaze ran over the small but tidy room; a definite upgrade from the classily furnished hotel lobby. The inside of Tom's suite was much more modern than I expected. The king-sized bed positioned between two tall windows sat low to the ground and the LED lights beneath the frame lit up the floor in a subtle shade of blue. On either side of the bed stood two acrylic nightstands with sleek metal lamps above each one. There was a massive television secured to the opposite wall and I could see a glimpse of a wide marble Jacuzzi tub in the slightly open bathroom door. I had to hand it to Isabella; she dropped some major cash on this place when she bought it from the previous owner.

To my right, Tom jiggled the ice in his glass, demanding my attention. "Would you like one?" he asked when I turned toward him.

"No, thank you. I'm driving."

The warlock downed the glass in a single gulp, then refilled it. "Suit yourself," he said breathlessly. "So, what brings you in this time? I'm not seeing a dinner tray."

"I'm not here to deliver food, I'm afraid," I said. My arms folded over my chest. *Though you could sure use it to sober up.* "I'm not sure how to say this, but I have some bad news about an old friend of yours."

Tom guffawed, throwing back another glass of whiskey. His glassy eyes focused and sharpened as they landed on me. "If you're here to tell me Linna died, I already know." He raised the empty cup. "Clearly."

Well, that at least explained the state Tom was in. I wondered if some of his excessive behavior could also be attributed to Isabella having gone missing. Probably, though I chose not to bring it up because I needed the man to come back to his senses if he was going to help me.

Uncrossing my arms, I walked toward the minibar in search of a coffee maker. Once I found it, I plugged in a coffee pod and turned it on, waiting for the hot liquid to fill a mug. Not bothering to ask Tom if he wanted it, I shoved the cup in his face and waited for him to accept. When he did, my shoulders relaxed a little.

"I'm sorry for your loss," I told the warlock. "I had only met Linna recently, but she seemed lovely."

For a member of an evil witch coven.

I left that part out.

Tom's brow furrowed and his gaze cast to the floor as he drank the coffee. "I didn't even know she was in Orchard Hollow. Why was she here? And at the beach, of all places?"

There was so much I could have said in that moment, but I chose my words wisely. I couldn't tell Tom why the Sister was in town, not without betraying her personal secrets. Dark magic witch or not, Linna didn't deserve to die, and she certainly didn't deserve for me to be gossiping about her love life. Especially not with the man it concerned.

I doubted adding guilt to Tom's already tragic state would do him much good.

"Why wouldn't Linna want to see the water?" I asked, choosing to focus on Tom's words instead.

He stood up taller. "Linna was deathly afraid of water," he explained. "Has been since we were kids. Here, look at this."

Taking a few strides, he crossed the room and reached for something on the nightstand. When he came to stand beside me again, he held out a cellphone with the gallery app pulled up. I looked at the warlock, then back to the screen and the photograph he pulled up. It was of a young boy and girl, standing together on a rocky beach in a town I didn't recognize. The girl was wrapped in a padded blanket and appeared to be soaked through. Beside her, the young boy was equally wet and had an arm around her protectively.

"Is that you two?" I asked, noting the similarity in the faces.

Tom nodded. "That was the last time Linna ever went swimming. The tide nearly took her. I had to jump in to haul her out and she vowed that she would forever hate swimming from that day forward." He looked at the picture, the corners of his eyes wrinkling. "Once Linna decided something, there was no talking her out of it."

That definitely sounded a lot like the woman I'd met. It also sounded an awful lot like Mrs. Cevil and it bugged me how alike the two witches were.

"Where were you here?" I asked.

"A private school in England," Tom said. "It's where we all met."

My lips tightened. "All?"

Tom pointed to the photo at the beach behind him and Linna. There was another boy in the shot, an awkward, lanky kid with a head full of blond hair and eyes that burned into the camera. My back grew rigid as I zoomed in on the boy's face and the scar across his one eyebrow. "Is that?"

"William Prude. That's him."

"I don't understand," I said, eyes glued to the photograph. "When you mentioned William the other day, you didn't say you were lifelong friends."

The warlock shrugged, tossing the phone on the bed. "Because we weren't. I haven't spoken to the guy in ages. But Linna stayed in touch, I believe." He walked back to the minibar and, surprisingly, reached for a bottle of water instead of the whiskey. "Come to think of it, I wonder if she was visiting him."

"It's possible," I lied. "How come you and William didn't stay in touch?"

"We never got along," Tom said. "He was a bit of an odd duck; always hanging around, but not really participating. You know the kind."

I nodded even though I didn't.

"And then there was his mother."

"His mother?"

The color started to return to Tom's face, and he was back to acting like the slimy salesman I remembered from before. He sat on the bed, reclining back suggestively. I fought back the vomit filling my throat.

"Very controlling," Tom said. "Poor Will had to check in with her constantly, which made him not so fun to be around. Anyway, we lost touch after school, and I have no intention of rekindling the friendship. Although now with Linna gone, I might have to track him down."

"I can give you his phone number if you'd like," I offered.

Tom waved me off dismissively. "I'll think about it." He quirked one eyebrow my way. "You still haven't told me why you came by."

There was no point dancing around it; best rip off the Band-Aid and see what happens. I puffed out my cheeks and met Tom's eyes.

"I don't think Linna drowned. I believe someone killed her. With magic," I added quickly. "I need your help to find the killer because I think it's the same person that killed Mrs. Cevil."

"I see," Tom said. "And why me?"

I pointed to the talisman ring on his finger.

The warlock swallowed, his Adam's apple bobbing up and down. "You need a warlock." He cocked his head to the side. "Witch?"

"Sort of," I answered. "There's a lot me and my friends can do, but it would be easier with your magic. The fact that you knew both victims will also help, a personal connection can help with tracking."

While all of that was true, there was one part I was leaving out. When fully energized, warlocks were incredibly powerful and if I could convince Tom to help, we might even be able to create a strong enough tracking spell to lead us straight to the killer. Or to the Sister responsible, as Mom insisted, and I was finally beginning to agree with. But that wasn't the only reason I wanted Tom's help. A part of me hoped that getting him involved would also get Isabella's attention if we were wrong about the Sisters and the vampire was behind this all along.

Either way, I couldn't lose with Tom on board.

"Will you help?" I asked again.

The warlock twisted his ring around once, twice, watching me intently. His beady eyes surveyed my face as he considered my suggestion. It was taking so long to respond that I started to lose all hope.

Finally, his lips twitched into a satisfied smile. "If I can help you find whoever did this to Linna, count me in. You'll need to get me close to a ley line."

I sagged against the wall.

"That I can easily do."

CHAPTER 22

It took a good hour to get Tom ready to leave. The man spent more time beautifying himself than I imagined Stella Rutherford did when she was alive, though, in his defense, twenty minutes were taken up by chugging two coffees to sober him up. By the time we were in Tom's Tesla and heading toward the farmhouse, I was so tired I couldn't stop yawning.

I glanced at my watch, shocked at the time of the night.

"You're lucky to live so close to the lines," Tom said as we veered onto the road leading past the woods. "So much energy here, I can already feel it."

I looked out the window at the dark skeletons of the trees on the horizon. "Really?"

"You don't feel that?"

"I'm not sure I have the same connection to the ley lines as you do," I said, another yawn escaping me.

The warlock looked past me through the window, his eyes dark and moody. "Right, witches don't need them as much. Even luckier." He brushed a loose strand of hair from his forehead, raking his fingers through his mane. "What's the plan, then?"

"Plan?"

"I assume you have an idea for finding the killer," Tom said. "Isn't that why we're here?"

My fingers flexed on the seat and I grabbed hold of the handle as the car came to a stop. Stepping out, I waited for Tom to join me outside. "My Mom has a spell she wants the three of us to try," I told the warlock when we reached the porch. "It's an incantation that, when combined with the right magical energy, should show us the traces of magic in town."

"A magical live map of sorts," Tom guessed.

"Something like that. We have to be careful with the wording of the incantation, but hopefully adding your warlock energy helps strengthen the connection."

Walking up the steps with Tom on my heels, I reached the front door and turned to face him. "Mom should be here any second. She can explain better," I said.

"Because it's her spell?"

I nodded. *And because I don't know how to explain it without telling you we're actually tracking a member of a witch coven your friend belonged to that might or might not want to end the world.* I knocked on the door to hurry my mother up.

As I did, the front door swung open and my balance gave way. I toppled backward, my shoulders smashing into the person on the other side. Laughing, my mother caught me and steadied me on my feet before I took both of us down. The warmth of her thick coat enveloped me and if it wasn't for everything we had to do, I'd have wanted to stay there forever. For the first time since mom showed up on my doorstep, I didn't want to shake off the thoughts. What I wished was to hang on to them for as long as possible. I didn't know if it was because I missed her or because we were quite literally running out of time. With Tom's help and assuming the spell worked, we should be able to track down Mrs. Cevil and Linna's killer. Then get to work on stopping the coven.

But what happened after?

Should we succeed, what would happen to Mom and me? Somehow, I doubted she would stick around. Despite all she said, getting out of Orchard Hollow wasn't only for my protection. A woman like my mother couldn't stay in one place for too long and I had the distinct feeling that when all of this was over, we'd be saying our goodbyes once again.

"Ready to start, honey?" Mom asked from behind me.

I steadied myself in more ways than one. "Sure thing," I whispered. "Lead the way."

"There's one thing we need to collect before we can cast the circle." My mother looked at Tom over my shoulder. "Any chance you might have anything that belonged to our dear Linna? Any object will do as long as she had contact with it. A connection to both victims would be helpful and I already have Reeba's favorite pen. Oh, and pleasure to meet you. I'm Sylvie."

She extended her hand and Tom shook it gracefully, his eyes twinkling at the sight of my mom. For a man whose girlfriend is missing and whose friend recently died, he sure had no problem flirting. Goosebumps ran up and down my arms, and I shivered. Did Tom know Isabella hadn't been accounted for in the last few days? Surely he would have if they were close. I was itching to ask him but there was no way to broach the subject without letting the warlock know I suspected her involvement and since we needed his help, I didn't want to rock the boat.

Maybe I could gather more information from him after we finished tonight.

The warlock let go of Mom's hand and patted his jacket aimlessly. "I'm afraid I don't. Will it be a problem?"

"Perhaps..." Mom said.

"What about the charm she left behind?" I asked.

Mom's head shook furiously and I felt a big no approaching. "It can't be a magical item," she said. "The energy will interfere with the spell and we can't afford to mess this up."

Well, that was a bust. Unless... An idea popped into my head and I held up a finger, excited to help. "I know where she was staying," I said. "And I know the owner of the bed and breakfast; she's a regular in the cafe. I might be able to get us one of Linna's belongings."

Catching sight of the empty driveway, I groaned, remembering the Beetle was out of commission until the end of the week. "Shoot. No car."

"Take mine," Tom offered and dangled his car keys in my face. "I can get started on tapping into the lines while you're gone. That is, if your lovely mother doesn't mind the company."

I reached for the keys reluctantly, trying not to make a face as I watched Tom wiggle his bushy brows at Mom. Thank the latte she didn't appear to care for his obnoxious come-hither stares and kept her focus only on me.

"It's getting late," she said. "Better get a move on if we want to get this over with before sunup."

Nodding, I left them on the porch and jogged toward Tom's Tesla. My heart raced in my chest as I neared the shiny vehicle. I had never driven anything this over the top and my body screamed in revolt as I climbed into the driver's seat. *What if I accidentally drove into a ditch?*

My pulse thundered in my head as I waited for the car to start, an urgency thrumming through me.

"Try not to crash the beauty."

I screamed, my hands gripping the steering wheel. Sweat pooled under my arms as I slowly turned around to face the passenger seat where my ghost familiar lounged comfortably. Stella's lips puffed out as she breathed, making them appear even larger. If that was possible.

"What are you doing here?" I shrieked, sucking in quick breaths.

The ghost winked. "You didn't think I'd miss the ride, did you?" she asked. "Who would pass up the chance to feel a proper engine roar to life?"

"I didn't realize you were such a car buff."

"I'm a luxury buff, darling," Stella corrected. "Now step on it and let's have some fun!"

To the dismay of my familiar, I did not in fact step on it. What I did was drive slower than the speed limit

— much, much slower— all the way to the bed and breakfast. When we arrived, I inspected the car for any possible damage before peeling my eyes away from the shiny black metal.

The bed and breakfast was exactly as I remembered it, a house plucked out of a fairy tale and deposited in our quaint town. The garden sitting behind the white picket fence was thriving despite it being one of the colder months. As I walked up the winding cobblestone path leading to the entrance, I couldn't help but smile at the massive round door that took up most of the front porch. Above it, a shingled awning directed my gaze toward the small windows with pink shutters and flower beds under each one. Ivy trailed up the side of the home all the way to the roof; painted the same shade of pink as the shutters.

As I walked toward the entrance, my gaze flashed to the other car parked in the driveway, one I recognized instantly.

"Hmm," I said between clenched teeth.

Behind me, Stella Rutherford paused. "What's that?"

"Looks like Linna's car. I recognize it from the other night."

I continued my journey up the walkway, praying it wasn't too late to show up unannounced. Miss Nolan was welcoming, but she was an older woman and I doubted she stayed up all night. While it was a reasonable hour, we were fast encroaching on rude-to-visit territory, and I was quickly regretting my choice to come here.

A whistle sounded at my back. I dug my heels into the ground and turned around.

"Come see this," Stella yelled out, her head poking out from behind Linna's sedan.

I glanced back at the house, then at my familiar. "What is it?"

The ghost didn't reply and only waved her hand faster, a sour expression on her face. She'd never leave me alone if I didn't agree to her demands and while I was running out of time, it was best to do as she said than to spend the next hour arguing with a spoiled ghost on Miss Roland's front steps.

My pace a fast click, I rushed toward her, stopping a foot away from the car's trunk.

Its slightly ajar trunk.

"Is that...?"

"Suspiciously open?" Stella asked. "Seems to be."

My wide eyes met Stella's. "Should we...?"

"Definitely."

Hand trembling, I grabbed the trunk's handle, taking my sweet time to open it. The door creaked as it lifted and I was hit with a stench so foul, it nearly knocked me off my feet. Bile shot up my throat and I pressed a hand to my mouth to stop from throwing up. Blue magic swirled over my fingers as the sense of danger enveloped me.

The glow of the magic lit up the inside of the trunk and my skin cooled. Beside me, Stella let out another low whistle.

I turned my head away, putting distance between myself and Linna's car. Still shaking, I reached for my phone. My vision spotted as I dialed the main number for the Orchard Hollow police station. The line rang one, twice, then a man's voice greeted me on the other end.

"Hi, Sheriff," I said.

"Miss Addison? What has you calling the station this late?" Romero asked.

I battled the urge to look back at the car. The magic on my fingers continued to pulse as I struggled to make words come out of my mouth. "You need to get down to Miss Nolan's," I finally uttered. "I think I found your missing body."

CHAPTER 23

I stood a ways back to give the sheriff and his team space to collect Mrs. Cevil's body. Across the street, Stella leaned against the trunk of a nearby tree, her blue eyes following the movements of the people gathered on the bed and breakfast's front lawn. Since it was fairly late and the funeral home director couldn't make it out, paramedics had to help transport the body to the city morgue until proper arrangements could be made. There was no doubt in my mind that Romero would want to gather evidence from the body though I doubted he would find anything useful.

Not far from me, Miss Nolan handed out steaming mugs of coffee to anyone willing to accept one. She spun from side to side to make sure she didn't miss anyone, her short blonde hair not moving an inch as she did. From what I recalled, there was usually at least one can of hairspray in that hair for as long as I had known the woman. Gran used to tell me to hide the matches when she came by to avoid a nuclear explosion. It was reassuring to know that despite everything, things were very much the same when it came to some people.

I waved meekly when she spotted me on the grass. My mood deflated more and more by the passing second; there was no way for me to get something that belonged to Linna now. Not with so many people here.

After speaking with one of the officers, the sheriff made his way across the lawn toward me. His face was unreadable. I rolled my shoulders back and straightened my posture as he approached, feeling like a child about to be scolded.

"Miss Addison," he said, tipping his hat in my direction.

I grimaced. "Hi again. Quite the night, huh?"

"You sure have a knack for finding dead bodies," the sheriff noted. "At least this time it's for the best and I can close a case."

Blanching, I folded my arms over my chest and looked at him. "Close which case?"

"Both," he answered. "It's obvious what happened here."

"It is?"

Romero signaled to the paramedics, and they slammed the doors of the ambulance shut, obscuring my view of the body bag. Not that I was complaining because, as the sheriff pointed out, I had my fair share of seeing dead bodies. When the ambulance pulled away and sped down the street, he returned his attention to me. "Of course," the sheriff said. "Linna Cruller killed Reeba in a heated argument, then drowned. Toxicology showed alcohol in her system and I don't have to tell you the dangers of being on our beaches at night while intoxicated. The sea does not mess around. Sometimes the simplest explanation is the most obvious one."

What the sheriff was saying was true, with one very big exception. In this particular case, the simplest explanation involved magic. My tongue itched from wanting to tell Romero how wrong he had it.

I couldn't.

If the sheriff thought he had his killer, he would leave the entire matter alone, which would take the attention off him. The best thing I could do for Romero and the entire Orchard Hollow police department— the *human* police department— was to keep my mouth shut. With the sheriff closing the case, he would stop poking around and hopefully not get a bull's eye on his back that would lead the Sisters of the River, or Isabella, straight to him.

"Why do you think Linna did it?"

The words left my lips before I could stop them. I mentally slapped myself for the slip, but the damage was done. I hoped it didn't stir any doubt in the sheriff and was relieved when he didn't appear to be shaken in the least.

Romero hitched a thumb, pointing to the bed and breakfast. "We found bank slips for large sums of money in Reeba's name in Miss Cruller's belongings. It appears Reeba borrowed quite a bit from the woman. I have a witness that placed Cruller in the bakery on several occasions this week, which leads me to believe she came to collect on her loans. Reeba's bank account was down to its last pennies, so I doubt she'd be able to pay back what she owed."

"And you're gathering they argued over it and Linna killed her?"

Romero frowned. "People have killed for less, I'm afraid."

I glanced at the house and watched as the owner of the establishment went inside to get more coffee for the group. The loan slips must have been from Tom's loans. The real killer would have had to snatch them from Mrs. Cevil's bakery in order to plant them on

Linna, which meant they had access to both the bakery and the bed and breakfast.

Either the Sisters thought of everything or they had a local helping them out.

I narrowed my eyes, intrigue crawling up my body. "Who was the witness that saw the two together?" I asked the sheriff.

"A handyman who worked at the bakery from time to time," he said. "William Prude."

Adrenaline carved up my spine, and I tried to keep a straight face as best as I could. Inside, a gut feeling began to bubble. Perhaps I was too quick to rule William out. Yet his motive did not make sense to me, mainly because he didn't have one. William was human and whoever killed Linna used magic to do it—witch magic. Unless William was a witch in disguise, there was no way he could be responsible.

Then why did I the hair on my arms stand on end?

It was no coincidence that he knew both victims—I was certain of it.

"Well, if you don't need me anymore, I'd better get going," I said a little too eagerly. "Thank you for filling me in."

"Miss Addison," the sheriff said quickly, "there is one more thing I wanted to check with you. I heard you had an unlucky incident yourself this evening. Anything I should know about?"

I bristled. "You mean the fire? Word really travels in this town."

"It sure does," the sheriff agreed. "So... do I need to be worried?"

"About me? Not at all. It was an accident, that's all. Everyone is safe, if not a little shaken up."

The sheriff studied me from behind the brim of his hat, his lips twitching. "I can send a car by every so often if you'd like."

He knows I'm lying. Why am I so bad at this? Refusing to cave in, I put on my best Sylvie smile and said, "Honestly, it was nothing. Please don't waste anyone's time on us. The only thing that suffered was the side of the house and it's nothing a little cleaning and elbow grease won't fix. I promise."

"All right. You have yourself a good night, Miss Addison. Call the station if you change your mind about the patrol car."

As I watched the sheriff walk away, I couldn't help but feel terrible. I hated lying to the man, even if it was for his own good. Vowing to tell Romero everything once it was safe to do so, I shuffled back to Tom's car, readying for the nerve-wracking ride back to the farmhouse.

My head spun around in search of Stella, who'd managed to perform another untimely disappearing act. For someone who acted like she hated the raccoon, she and Harry Houdini had a lot in common. An image of Stella digging through a garbage can flashed in my mind and I laughed out loud, opening the car door to climb in.

Before I could make it, a blue light shimmered to my left, and I paused, turning slowly to follow the glimmer. A few feet from me, the air rippled and began to tear into two, a seam opening. I opened my mouth to scream for help, then closed it quickly. I was in the middle of a residential street late at night, surrounded by humans. Who did I think was going to assist me?

My eyes darted behind me for a final check on Stella. *Still gone.* Wonderful.

The rift doubled in size, and the darkness within it seemed almost palpable. As before, a shadow scurried across, making me jump. Whatever was in there, it was alive.

Working against my better judgment, I made my way toward the growing tear, my legs quaking the entire time. When I was close enough to reach out and touch it, I stopped dead in my tracks. My heart beat wildly and cold sweat licked the skin at the base of my back. Toes curled, I swallowed the lump in my throat, tilting my head to the side to see deeper into the abyss before me. My entire body shook as an invisible energy grabbed hold of me and pulled me in. I dug my heels in, but it was as though my body and my brain wanted different things.

Reluctantly, I stepped closer. The smell of pickle juice wafted into my nostrils and I wiggled it to prevent a sneeze. There was a hint of a spice I couldn't put my finger on as well and the combination of the two was nauseating.

"Hello, Piper," a deep voice boomed from inside the tear.

My eyes rounded.

"Don't be shy," the voice purred. "Come a little closer. Let's have a look at you."

I shook my head back and forth, willing the rift to close. It remained open, though it stopped growing in size. "Who are you? How do you know my name?"

The sound of laughter filled the air between me and the darkness. I wiped my glistening brow, waiting for a reply.

"I know a lot more than names, darling," the voice said.

"Who are you?" I insisted.

Another fit of laughter rose from within and this time, I wasn't paralyzed by it. Whatever was on the other side of the tear was beginning to annoy me and I didn't have the patience to deal with the frustrating creature within. I had my own problems to deal with.

Widening my stance, I called forth my magic. It

ran across my skin, electricity thrumming at the tips of my fingers. The corners of my lips lifted as they peeled back into a sneer. "Didn't anyone teach you it's not polite to laugh at people?" I asked. "Time to go bye-bye."

I pushed my magic outward, ready to repeat what Mom helped me do at the bakery to close the rift. The voice spoke again as I did, and I stopped what I was doing instantly.

"You look like your mother," it said. "Though you have my eyes. His eyes."

What in the latte? My temples throbbed as I tried to make sense of what the creature said. There was only one explanation, but I refused to believe it. It couldn't be. My hands dropped to my sides, limp. "Who are you?"

"There will be plenty of time for that," the voice said. "Until we meet again."

Then the rift closed. I was surrounded only by the cold fresh air of an Orchard Hollow night. My stomach tensed, knees buckling as a tremor of fear sliced through me. Leaning against the car for support, I climbed into the driver's seat and sped back to the farmhouse. I was returning empty-handed, but I didn't much care. There would be no spells performed tonight; I had another agenda set now. It was time for mother dearest to come clean.

CHAPTER 24

"Where's Tom?" I asked, watching my mother walk through the front door and close it behind her.

She fastened the lock before stepping over to the large bay window in the living room and drawing the curtains shut. When she was satisfied, she came to sit beside me on the couch. "I left him in the woods," Mom answered. "The man is obsessed with the ley lines. I figured he may as well keep himself busy, since we won't be performing the tracking spell tonight."

"We can try asking the sheriff for Linna's things later," I said. "I'm sure he'll have all her belongings bagged for evidence now that he suspects her of killing Mrs. Cevil."

"Foolish man," Mom said, clucking her tongue.

An awkward silence filled the living room as we sat across from each other. My arm draped on the side of the couch and I played with the fringe on one of Gran's pillows, avoiding Mom's eyes. I didn't know why it was so hard for me to ask her what I wanted to know. I had every right to the truth and yet I found myself idling, waiting for any excuse to avoid the subject.

A memory of the voice in the rift flashed in my mind and I shuddered. *Stop wasting time. Rip the Band-Aid off.*

"So," I uttered quietly. "There was an incident tonight, one that I need you to explain."

Mom's forehead creased with worry. "Please tell me you didn't find someone else dead."

"Not exactly. When I was leaving the bed and breakfast, another rift opened."

"Did you close it? Did anything get out?"

The fringe fell between my fingers as I stopped breathing to look at her. "Comments like that are the reason we need to have this talk," I said. "Care to explain why something, or someone, on the other side of the rift talked to me tonight? Or why he implied he might be my father?"

"How about a drink?" Mother asked.

I yanked her back down before she had a chance

to escape. "I don't think so. No more secrets. What's going on, Mom?"

Taking her sweet time, she settled into a comfortable position. Her long legs crossed into a lotus shape pose and she leaned on her knees, drawing her elbows in until they almost touched. *Someone has been practicing their yoga.* I tried to mimic her, but ended up nearly dislocating both my shoulders.

If Stella were here, I'd never hear the end of it.

Where is that ghost, anyway?

"I suppose it was bound to come out sooner or later," Mom said, interrupting my looking around the room in search of my familiar. "I always knew he would find you. Damn it."

I sank deeper into the couch cushions. "Then it's true? Whatever was inside the rift was what? My dad?"

"Dad is a stretch. Think of him as more of a donor."

"First of all, ew. Second—" I paused to think. "You know, there is no second. Gross, Mom. Can you explain without the visuals, please?"

Mom's hands shot up in defense. "All right, all right. You're so touchy." She rolled her eyes. "Remember when I explained that the Sisters needed a vessel to summon Hades?"

"Vaguely. You didn't explain all that well, to be honest."

"I was hoping you would stop asking," she admitted. "Guess you're more like me than I realized. Well, the vessel isn't an object. It's a human. They need a person to place Hades' entity into so he could cross from the Underworld to our realm on Earth."

I fisted my fingers, then spread them wide atop my knees, trying to keep up. "Let me guess. Malachi? It would make sense to use a descendent of the ancient God as a vessel. Poetic almost." Thinking back to what she'd told me before, I asked, "I thought you said they'd never been able to succeed?"

Mom's eyes darted to side, and she bit her bottom lip. Her nervousness was so thick it was palpable. Despite everything, she was still trying to keep things from me.

"What is it?" I asked, scowling.

"The thing of it is," Mom started, "the Sisters managed to open a doorway before but only briefly. When that happens, Hades basically gets sucked back in. But not before..."

My throat was suddenly tight and full. "Before what?"

"Let's say they have successfully put the bastard into Malachi," Mom said. Her cheeks reddened, and she scratched her chest like she was breaking out in hives. "You have to believe me, though, honey. I had no clue it was him until it was too late."

Blinking, I stared at her as I struggled to connect the dots. Shifting uncomfortably before me, Mom's face continued to heat up until she was so red she resembled a ripe tomato. My mouth gaped as the realization of what she was telling me started to creep in.

"Hold on," I said, wrapping my head around the concept. "Are you telling me that Malachi was actually Hades when you two... did things?"

Mom nodded.

I swallowed the bile filling my mouth.

"Oh, sweet coffee," I whispered. "She was right."

"Who was?"

Shrugging, I covered my eyes with the palm of hand, an exasperated sigh escaping me. "Stella. Never mind that. I seriously can't believe this. My father is an ancient deity. Is that even possible? How?" I had many questions. Stopping myself from falling over the edge, I removed my hand and looked at Mom. "You know, don't tell me. I don't think I can handle those details right now. But I don't understand, I found letters from Malachi to you. He sounded like he was trying to help you and Gran bind my Underworld magic."

"He was," Mom answered. "He was quite sweet. Tried to do right by us after he found out I was pregnant with you."

"If he was so great, how come I never met him?"

Tears welled in Mom's eyes, and she swiped at them with her palms, blinking away incoming tears. I braced myself for bad news, as usual. "When the coven first performed the ritual, no one realized it worked. Malachi and I only discovered what happened by accident and by then it was too late to help him. The energy of Hades— it was too strong. It broke him. So much so that it was impossible to survive it."

"He died? That's why you were using his picture when you cast the dark magic to draw the Sisters out, isn't? Because summoning the dead is pretty much the darkest magic there is."

Looking down into her lap, Mom sniffled, playing with her nails as she fought back tears. Whatever happened with her and Malachi, she cared for the man. I wondered how much of that was because he tried to protect me and how much was another reason entirely, perhaps even real love. A part of me was crushed to find out I would never meet the man who made me, but another part, the part that was livid, knew Malachi wasn't my father at all. As Mom said, he was a vessel. My real dad was the thing of nightmares.

Another thought jumped to the surface. I gasped.

"Do you think that's why I can see Stella? Because my dad is quite literally the God of Death?"

"It's possible," Mom admitted. "It would also explain your extracurricular activities."

"What do you mean?"

She walked toward the kitchen, my eyes following her every move. Pulling out a stemless wine glass, Mom poured herself a glass of cabernet and leaned over the counter. She twirled the wine slowly, sniffing at the edge of the cup. "Didn't you even wonder why you keep finding yourself in these morbid situations?" she asked, taking a long sip. "You must be the only person in the history of Orchard Hollow to stumble upon dead bodies like it was going out of style."

"You think it's because of my magical heritage?"

"Of course!" Mom exclaimed. "You, my dear, are a magnet for death. Like father, like daughter, I suppose."

I growled. "Marvelous."

"Hey, it's not all bad news. Look at you and Stella. I have to say, you make quite the pair and to think you'd be stuck with a cat if you were a regular witch."

Chuckling, I pointed to the bottle of wine and patted the empty couch seat beside me. Mom grabbed a second glass and filled it halfway before dragging herself over to join me. We drank in silence as I wrapped my head around everything she said. It was, for lack of a better word, unbelievable. Yet it did explain quite a bit about the recent events in my life and even more about my magic.

Holy coffee bean. I'm half Hades. Wow!

"You know who would get a kick out of all this?" Mom asked.

I lowered one brow in question.

"You grandmother," she said. "When I first suggested we bind your magic to hide you from your father and the Sisters, she wanted nothing to do with it."

"Why not?"

Mom shrugged, putting her cup down on the coffee table. "I think she thought it wasn't fair to force the decision on you. That you should have been the one to make it."

"I take it you didn't agree?"

"You were a child, Piper. The Sisters were dangerous and your father, well, he was a brand new level of scary. I didn't want you anywhere near them knowing what they intended to do."

Cold fingers wrapped around my heart as I understood what she was hinting at. "If the Sisters found out I existed, they'd use me as their next vessel."

"I couldn't let them get to you," Mom whispered. "Even if it meant I wasn't going to be around to see you grow up. You have to admit, I didn't completely mess things up."

"Ha!" I guffawed. "How do you figure?"

"For starters, I kept you hidden for all these years. And the world is intact, so that's a win." She sighed. "If your grandmother could bear witness to us now..."

My heart stopped. "What did you say?"

"About hiding you?"

"No, the part about bearing witness," I corrected. "You reminded me of what the sheriff said. He mentioned that William Prude saw Linna hanging around the bakery."

"William? How would he even know who Linna was? She wasn't a local."

Toes curling in my socks, I stretched out my legs to give my nerves something to do. Doing my best not to leave anything out, I told her everything Tom revealed about his childhood and the three musketeers. It was strange to think that they all ended up in our town at the same time, unless it wasn't a lucky break. Or not so lucky for Linna.

Mom must have been thinking the same thing.

I bit off a loose hangnail while she studied my every move. Leaning over, she wiggled her brows, asking, "Do you still have that folder the werewolf gave you?"

"Yes," I said cautiously. "Why?"

Mom smiled mischievously. "I'll tell you, but you're not going to like it."

With that, she stood up and made her way to the door. Draping her coat over her shoulders, she opened the door and welcomed the cold into the house. Mom turned to look at me. Despite my better judgment, I stood up and followed her lead. Whatever she had planned, I would surely pay for it later.

With a sigh, I left my half-drunk glass of wine on the entrance table and followed my mother into the night.

CHAPTER 24

Here we go again.

We stood cloaked by the dead of night in front of a small bungalow on the edge of town. The roof of the house was slightly slanted, and the shingles looked like they had seen better days. Surrounding the front porch were more weeds than grass, and there was a crack in one of the windows where something appeared to have hit it.

To sum up, the house was one of the more rundown properties in Orchard Hollow.

I peered left and right, uneasy with the lack of other homes on the dead-end street. At our back, the woods that took up most of this part of town covered the land and obscured us from the view of the main road. If I were to scream, I doubted anyone could hear us for miles.

"This doesn't look like a place William would live," Mom said.

Grudgingly, I had to agree with her. Glancing at the map on my phone, I double checked the address Ember gave me. "It's the right address," I told her. "He mentioned his Mom moving out of town. Maybe this was his childhood home, and he has another place now."

"Maybe," Mom whispered. Somehow, I doubted she believed me. Brushing down the hairs of her wool coat, she checked the front porch and the lack of light around it. "Doesn't look like anyone is home. Let's go."

Feet unmoving, I traced her steps with my eyes as she walked toward the front door. Moving like a freaking ninja, Mom lowered to a half-crouch when she approached the house and veered to the side. She skirted the building, waving for me to join, before disappearing around the bend. The overgrown bushes circling the house made it impossible to see her, and I huffed out a frustrated breath before following her lead.

One of these days, this woman was going to get us arrested for her antics. Since when was breaking and entering a regular part of her repertoire? I wasn't sure what skills Mom picked up while with the Sisters but it seemed this was one of them.

I did not like it one bit.

Rounding the side of the house, I patted my jacket pocket to make sure my phone was still there, relieved when I felt the outline of it with my fingers.

Get in, get out. Go home, I told myself.

A loud whack pierced the air, and I jumped at the sound.

"Got it!" Mom whisper-screamed from somewhere in the distance.

I crept closer to her voice, one foot in front of the other and keeping my balance on my toes to stop them from making any noise. Neck twisting, I continued to watch out for people, even though I knew there was no one else here but us. It was moments like this that I wished I had a better way of summoning my familiar. Stella's ghostly skills would be perfect for the operation Mom had planned. It was a shame she wasn't around when we left tonight.

When all of this was over, I needed to find a solution to our broken communication.

Taking another unsure step forward, I stopped when my eyes finally adjusted to the light and I could see Mom in front of me. She held a metal crowbar in one hand and looked down into the depths of the cellar doorway she pried open. I frowned as I approached. "Do you ever follow the law?"

"You can pass your judgment on my morals later," she said, taking the first step down. "Let's see if your hunch is correct before someone comes home."

A hand reached out to yank me down. I stutter-stepped down the creaky stairs after Mom, my gait unsteady, trying my best not to fall forward as we made our way into the cellar. The moonlight provided a tiny sliver of sight as it streamed from behind us, but it was nearly impossible to make out where we were. The smell of mold and wet soil made me realize not seeing was probably for the best.

My feet hit level ground, and I breathed out the breath I was holding. It only took Mom a second to orient herself and she was back to pulling me behind her as she rushed up a second set of stairs leading up into the main house.

"How do you know where to go?" I whispered.

"All these old houses are the same," Mom said. "Once you've been to one, you can pretty much find your way around with your eyes closed."

How lucky. Walking blindly was exactly what we were doing.

Mom navigated us up the stairs like a SWAT team member. Before I knew it, we were on the main floor and she was using her phone's flashlight to show us around. "Let's check here," she said, tugging on my sleeve.

Turning on my phone to provide more light, I stayed on her heels as she dragged me to a closed door past the small kitchen. Despite the outside appearance of the house, it was much cozier in here than I imagined. The floor under our feet was freshly lacquered, the walls were painted a bright shade of eggshell, and there was a smell of baked pie in the air; as if someone had been here recently.

Mom looked at me over her shoulder, then twisted the knob, pushing the door open. We stood a foot away from the entrance and checked around the room before finally venturing in.

"A bedroom," Mom said.

I glanced at the carefully made bed in the center of the room. "Nothing sinister here."

Shutting the door behind us, we continued our search of the house, taking note of every detail that pointed to William. There were a few framed photos of him at different ages hanging on the walls at odd intervals. One I recognized to be the same timeline as the photo Tom showed me in his hotel room. This must have been right before he was sent off to school, where he met Tom and Linna.

We checked two more rooms with the same outcome as the first— another bedroom and a walk-in closet full of boxes and random household items. So far, William's childhood home reminded me more of the farmhouse than the lair of an evil mastermind. Mom veered to the right and down a narrow hallway leading to the bathroom while I started for the back-yard. She was almost out of sight when something caught my attention.

"Mom, wait," I said, calling her back. My finger pointed to the etchings on the wall surrounding a small cabinet. "Look."

Angling her phone to face the wall, Mom's nose scrunched as she leaned forward to study the carvings. "Concealment runes."

"But William is human."

We exchanged glances, and I took a step back while Mom pulled out a sprig of rosemary from her purse. She crushed the leaves in her hand, then rubbed them on the runes, throwing her magic outward. The runes lit up a bright purple that faded instantly. As they dimmed, the cabinet changed shape before my eyes. No longer was it a standard console table; in its place stood a large, mahogany armoire with wide double doors lined in bronze.

Reaching out, Mom grabbed one door while I took the other and we pulled. As the cabinet swung open, our jaws unhinged.

"It's a—"

"Witch's wardrobe," I said. "Why would William have it here?"

My fingers grazed the trinkets on the shelves, my body reacting to their magical properties on contact. The wardrobe was so similar to the one Gran had back home I could have sworn they were a twin set. Perhaps William collected old wardrobes and didn't know what he had on his hands? I felt foolish the second I thought about it. Even if William Prude was an antique collector— an unlikely coincidence— there would be no need for him to keep magical items used for spells and potions. Nor would he know how to use concealment runes to hide the bulky thing from prying eyes.

Eyes catching on an object out of place, I paused and reached for the bright pink designer wallet on one shelf. My stomach dropped and my breath left me as I opened it. The wallet had a wad of cash in it and there were a few cards in the slots that gave me the impression it belonged to someone very well off. I pulled out one card and gasped.

"Oh no," I told Mom. "This is Isabella Beaumont's wallet."

"The vampire?" Mom asked.

I nodded, continuing to check the rest of the wardrobe. Tucked in the corner behind a few potion bottles was an old photograph. The edges had curled from age and it was yellowing in different spots across the glossy surface. I brought it up to my face, recognizing the face of the young man in it. "It's William," I said and handed Mom the picture. "With his mom."

There was a long silence and for a brief moment, I thought Mom left me behind and ran off. Turning slowly, I faced her, my body stilling when I registered the fear on her face.

I placed a hand on her shoulder, shaking it lightly. "What's wrong?"

"William's mother," Mom said. "She's in the coven, Piper. She's a head witch for the Sisters of the River."

Headlights came alive from the front of the house, shining a spotlight on our garish faces through the living room window. I looked past Mom into the hallway, biting the inside of my cheek.

We were no longer alone.

CHAPTER 24

Back pressed to the wall, I tracked the woman's movements as she strode towards us. The light from two car headlights streamed in through the living room window behind her, illuminating her in a yellow halo and making her frizzy hair glimmer at the edges. From where I stood, it was difficult to make out her age, though if I had to try, I'd place her to be older than Mom but younger than Gran. She wore a long, tailored coat over a knit jumpsuit that touched the floor as she walked.

The woman took a few more steps, and my ears thrummed from the sound of her boots squeaking against the hardwood floor. I stared into her cold, gray eyes, bile swirling in my stomach.

"I knew you were tricky," William's mother said, her gaze locked on Mom.

Standing between me and the witch, my mother scoffed, the sound akin to a slap in the face. "Right back at you, Cassandra."

My eyes flicked to the photo in my hands. Cassandra and William Prude standing side by side, mother and son. So this was the woman William casually mentioned in our conversation. I wanted to kick myself for not putting the pieces together, but how was I supposed to know William's mom was a witch? And a Sister of the River at that. Her son was so human that it never even occurred to me to check.

Even Mom was surprised by the turn of events.

"I thought the last name seemed familiar," she said. "You don't go by it anymore, though. What is it now? Holder?"

Cassandra sneered, and it made her appear even creepier than she already was. Her skin stretched as she spread her thin lips wider to reveal a set of uneven teeth. "Prude was my married name. I left it behind with the man it belonged to."

"Kill that one too?" Mom asked.

I coughed into my hand and nudged her in the ribs with my elbow. Was she trying to get us cursed by a head witch? Now that we stood here in William's childhood home, I had no doubt that either he or his mom were responsible for what happened to Mrs. Cevil and Linna. They may have even worked together. If Mom didn't keep her mouth shut, we'd be following in the footsteps of the other witches this duo took out and I was intent on walking out of here alive tonight.

"Or do you only enjoy killing other witches?" Mom added.

There goes my plan of surviving...

I jabbed her again, stopping when Cassandra laughed. The witch wiped her eyes and looked at my mother playfully. "Honestly, Sylvie, you were always so dramatic," she said.

"Tell me," Mom continued. "Would you describe what you did to my friend and your own coven member as dramatic? Because I can think of a few better words."

"As I said, very dramatic."

Gaze turning thunderous, Mom fisted her hands and pounded her left one into the adjoining wall. The hit reverberated across the drywall, causing the picture frames to shake. "Damn it, Cassandra! Why?"

"You know quite well why," Cassandra replied coolly. "Or did you think you were clever, plotting your little coup behind the coven's back?"

My face blanched, and I reached for Mom's hand, but she brushed me away. Stepping forward, she angled her body to shield me from the witch, her eyes narrowing. "Why didn't you come for me too?" she asked, her voice hoarse.

"Honestly, I wasn't sure you were involved. Not until tonight when I saw you scurry into my home." Her gaze caught on me. "You and your daughter. I suppose it best we find out now before you bring another traitor into the fold. Shame, I was hoping the fire would have scared you away, but here we are."

A loud bang pierced my ear drums as Mom pummeled another fist into the wall. This time, she didn't stop there. Her left hand reached into a jacket pocket and she yanked out a small item too quickly for me to see what it was. I guessed it was a sprig of wolfsbane to help summon her fire magic because the next thing I knew, she had a ball of fire floating over her open palm. Moving like lightning, Mom hurled the fireball at Cassandra before I had a chance to blink.

I gasped as the witch raised a hand and extinguished the magic in seconds.

"Please," Cassandra said, tsking, "let's not embarrass ourselves. You don't stand a chance against a head witch of my caliber."

A low growl shook Mom's chest as she asked, "Did she suffer?"

"Who? Your ancient friend?" Cassandra's eyes darkened a few shades as she rolled them over my mother. "Unfortunately, not as much as I'd have liked. Using magic was out of the question, so I had to get creative."

Beside me, Mom let out a low moan, and I felt her body sink into mine. I widened my stance to hold both our weights, a thought popping in my head out of nowhere. "It wasn't William who killed her?" I asked, speaking for the first time since Cassandra walked in.

"Of course not," she said. Head cocking to the side, she glanced between Mom and me. "The apple certainly stayed near the tree with her, didn't it? It's a shame the coven has to lose two exceptional witches. You would have been a wonderful addition to the Sisters."

I looped around Mom and tugged her behind me before she could do something that would put us into even more trouble. Keeping Cassandra's focus on me, I said, "But he was the one that led the police to Linna. If he didn't help you kill them, surely he was still involved."

"Getting your kid to do your dirty work, Cassandra?" Mom asked. "Classy."

"You're one to talk," the witch rebutted, her chin pointing to me. "And William has no idea about any of this, so you leave him out of it. Though it was useful to have his connections and his keys to the bakery. My sweet boy is not too quick when it comes to women, but I have to admit, when he told me about you, Sylvie, it got me thinking. Why were you back here when you went on and on about how much you hated this town? What was it you called it? An anchor?"

Goosebumps spread over my arms at her words. I knew that Cassandra was trying to get under Mom's skin by upsetting me and I wished I didn't give her the satisfaction of enjoying it, but my emotions were clear on my face. I guessed that Mom despised Orchard Hollow but to hear someone else say it, a stranger, made it that much more real. If she hated our town, she must have hated me and Gran too. Otherwise, why leave? Why not stay so we could handle the problems we faced as a family?

To say I had mommy issues was the understatement of the century.

Refusing to let the witch get to me any further, I pushed aside my demons and concentrated on what she said. I couldn't believe what I was hearing. This woman had used her own son to help her in her vile actions, going so far as to use his keys to Mrs. Cevil's bakery to steal the loan documents she held there so she could plant them on Linna. Didn't she think things through? What would happen if the sheriff could connect her son to the crimes? Stupid, selfish woman.

"Who's this now?"

I jumped at the sound of Stella's voice behind me.

Doing my best not to draw attention to the fact that we had company, or to look absolutely unhinged in front of the lunatic witch who was certainly gunning to kill us, I stayed stock still. Out of the corner of my mouth, I whispered, "Bad news. Thanks for coming."

A flash of movement from further down the hallway caught my eye, and I yelped as another fireball flew past me, its flames licking my skin. It smashed into the wall inches from Cassandra's head, leaving a dark burn mark behind. The witch smirked, her smile slanting toward my Mom.

"Your aim is improving," she said. "Not good enough, I'm afraid. Your baker friend was better."

Mom seethed, and I had to physically restrain her before she set the entire house on fire. From behind me, Stella said, "Let her at it," and slow clapped. I ignored the ghost, positioning Mom further from Cassandra. My eyes scanned the dimly lit house. I needed to buy time to plan an escape.

Facing the Sister head on, I fixed a serious glare on her and said, "There's something I don't understand. You killed Mrs. Cevil because she tried to put a stop to your coven and I'm assuming Mom would have suffered a similar fate when you finally figured out her involvement." I wanted to add myself into the mix but chose to stop there. "But why Linna? As Mom mentioned, wasn't she one of you?"

Heat flashed behind Cassandra's eyes as they darted away from me before landing on her feet. She bit her bottom lip, chewing it like one would an overcooked steak.

"Oh, my goddess," Mom whispered. "The other Sisters don't know you're here, do they? You thought you could handle it yourself and get a pat on the back. Perhaps climb a few ranks before the big ceremony on the next blood moon?"

Cassandra grit her teeth.

For the love of coffee, Mom was right.

I uncurled my spine to stand a little taller. "I take it the coven might have handled the situation differently," I guessed. "Perhaps even without all the violence. What happened? Did Linna figure out what you did and was going to rat you out to the other Sisters?"

"Ha!" the witch screeched. "She should have done that instead of trying to stop me herself. Who did she think she was going up against me? A junior witch taking on a head witch, what a joke."

Mom and I exchanged twin looks of worry, our fingers touching briefly for support. Head witch or not, the woman was absolutely off her rocker. Mom said the Sisters were power-hungry and dangerous, but it was starting to appear that even they wouldn't have gone on a murderous rampage. At least not without covering their butts; something Cassandra clearly forgot to do or else we wouldn't be standing here now.

I scowled, my body reeling. "So you killed one of your own to protect yourself?" I asked. "And then got your son to lie for you by pointing the finger at her to the sheriff."

"I already told you my sweet boy is not involved. All it took was some suggesting to convince him he truly did see Linna at the bakery. I knew sooner or later he wouldn't be able to help himself and spew the story around town." She smiled, pleased with herself. "He always did love a good story, that boy."

"And the award for Mother of the Year goes to..."

Stella rapped off a drumming sound on her thighs and rolled her eyes. I had to agree with her there. If you had asked me weeks ago who that award should go to, I'd have pointed you to Sylvie Addison. Yet right now, I couldn't picture a worse parent than the vicious witch standing before me.

A burst of pink drew my attention back to the wardrobe. My blood ran cold as I caught sight of Isabella's wallet, putting two and two together. Or, in this case, putting a vampire and a warlock together.

Turning my head, I sucked in a breath, steadying my shaking heart. "Isabella is gone too, isn't she?"

"Who?" Cassandra tilted her head to the side and

pulled at her memory. "You mean the vampire? Nasty little thing, that one was."

"Why her?" Mom asked, confused.

I lowered my head, my chin pressing to my chest. "Because she figured it out. I don't know how she did it, but between trying to buy out the bakery and her dating Tom, she must have found out about you."

"She did a bit more than that," Cassandra hissed. "The bloodsucker tried to come for me. Didn't work out well for her, not when I have this."

Reaching into the cowl of her sweater, the witch pulled out a long chain with a glass vial attached to it. Cassandra dangled it in front of us, her lips peeling back from her teeth. As she twirled the chain, the liquid in the vial began to glow a bright pink shade that reflected off her pale skin.

"Is that a fairy blessed potion?" Mom asked.

The witch nodded cockily.

"Wait one minute!" Stella raised a long finger. "Fairies are real?"

I bristled. "Sure are. Will tell you more later."

"Who are you talking to?" Cassandra asked. "You know what? It doesn't matter."

The next few seconds went by in a blur. It seemed a million things happened at the same time, and my focus was torn between the moving pieces. Something boomed from down the hallway and light exploded in my eyes, making it impossible to see clearly. My vision swam at the same time as Mom pushed me to the side and knocked me into the wardrobe. From behind us, Stella shrieked for Mom to watch out.

I landed on my side, groaning as the pain from the impact numbed my shoulder. My eyes unfocused as I tried to track my mother, following her to the middle of the hallway, a few feet away from Cassandra. She lay on her back, struggling to get up as a dark liquid oozed out of the wound in her leg.

Mouth opening and closing, I worked to make out her words, terror coursing through me when I did.

"Run!" my mother screamed.

At my back, Stella shouted the same thing, but louder. My head pounded, and I struggled to stand. I had to get to Mom. Another loud bang boomed down the hallway. My legs gave out from under me. I hit the hardwood floor like a sack of potatoes just in time to see Cassandra flick her wrist and throw her magic straight for me.

CHAPTER 24

Fire singed my hair. The smell of burning made my stomach roll. I twisted around in time to miss Cassandra's second hit; the fireball slamming into the wardrobe with a violent hit. The pain in my shoulder intensified and I felt as though my entire arm shattered into pieces like a mirror.

Seven years of bad luck.

Forcing my brain to focus, I flattened my palms on the floor and pushed up to kneel. My rubbery legs shook under the weight and I had to breathe through the pain to stand upright. Gaze searching the hallway, I spotted Mom crouching in an open doorway leading to one of the bedrooms we'd searched earlier. Her skin was the color of driven snow, but she was breathing and that was all that mattered.

Down the hall, Cassandra cast another fire spell and walked toward me, picking up speed quickly.

"Piper, get out!" Mom shouted.

Air hissed between my clenched teeth. "I'm not leaving you!"

I blindly reached into the wardrobe to grab a potion bottle, then threw it at Cassandra. The glass shattered a foot from her in a sparkling mess that dealt absolutely no damage. Overjoyed with my failure, the witch grinned toothily and threw the fireball she summoned at my head.

Ducking, I twisted my aching body to avoid the hit. My eyes roped to my idle fingers. *Where is my magic when I need it?*

"Use your powers," Stella suggested, crouching beside me. I wasn't sure why she needed to hide, but I supposed instinct stayed behind no matter how dead you were.

I gritted my teeth, my jaw clenching tightly. "I'm trying," I told the ghost. "It's not working."

Another burst of fire crashed a little too close to my butt, and I jumped, pain tearing through my arm from the sharp movement. I closed my eyes and reached for my magic again, but I couldn't feel it. Why was it so hard all the time? Maybe if I had something to anchor myself to.

Peeling my lids apart, I scanned Cassandra's clothing for any hint of a talisman; there was nothing in sight. I couldn't even feel her family's magic from here. Either the witch was strong, even without the help of a family talisman, or it was hidden somewhere I couldn't reach it. Either way, the plan to piggyback off her ancestral magic fizzled away. I was back at square one.

Another hit tore past my hair, burning it off. "Hey!" I yelled. "I didn't sign up for a haircut!"

"In her defense, you can certainly use one," Stella quipped in response.

"Now is not the time."

The ghost rolled her eyes, crawling toward me. "I'm going to try something," she said. "Don't get mad."

Before I could ask her what she meant, Stella jumped at me, knocking me backward. The impact sent me barreling into the side of an open doorway and my back cracked as it hit the wood. I was about to tell the ghost off when she met my eyes, winked, and shoved her ghost body into mine.

Stars exploded behind my lids and my mind raced

with panic as I lost control of my limbs. I willed myself to move, but nothing happened; I was me, but I wasn't me. Memories of when Stella tried this trick before resurfaced.

Why did she decide to possess me now? Last time it was so she could share some of her power with me because I was quite literally dying. But that wasn't the case now. Yes, I was getting my butt handed to me by a Sister but I wasn't doing too bad.

I willed for Stella to vacate my body, yet she wouldn't budge. *I'm not a vacation rental,* I seethed, working to expel the ghost.

Suddenly, my right arm lifted, and a palm came down on my cheek. Hard.

Did she seriously slap me with my own damn hand?

I swore to make Stella's afterlife a painful and horrible experience as she raised my left arm and repeated the slap. My head pounded from having too many thoughts in it, some of them not my own. In my periphery, the air rippled. I stopped fighting the ghost.

A rift, I thought.

"Finally," Stella said, standing over me. "I thought I was going to have to beat you senseless."

Realizing I was me again, I pressed my back to the doorway and used it to help me stand. Near to us, the rift grew larger and its presence seemed to have attracted Cassandra's attention, who put a pin in trying to kill me to stare into the deep void. My gaze jumped from her to Stella. "How did you know that would work?"

"I didn't," the ghost said with a shrug. "You're welcome."

My mouth opened to scold her, but she vanished before I could say a word. As she did, the rift rippled again and expanded to twice its size, as though Stella's presence was holding it back somehow. My fingers itched. I looked down to see them light up like Christmas trees with the blue magic I couldn't summon before. As I raised them, the sparks flew from my hands and into the rift, making it grow again.

Perhaps it wasn't Stella at all...

"What the hell is that thing?" Cassandra screeched.

I noticed she was keeping a good distance from the rift, the bravado she showcased before evaporating. My lips twitched into a half-smile. "You don't recognize your life's work?" I quipped.

The witch gasped.

"It can't be," she whispered. "But how?"

Pulling herself away from the tear, she looked in my direction, finally noticing the magic in my hands.

Her eyes bulged out of her head and her jaw slacked, hitting the floor.

"You."

I watched her do the math in her head until the realization of who I was showed on her face. Cassandra blinked rapidly, her chest rising and falling with quick, panicked breaths.

"Good to see you again, daughter," a deep voice rumbled from inside the tear in the air.

I groaned. "Not there yet with the nicknames," I hissed out. "Took you long enough to show up."

"You can thank your ghost for that. Let her know she's welcome to join us here," the voice, my deity father, said.

No wonder Stella hightailed it out of here. I was pretty sure that if she stayed, the rift would suck her up into oblivion. After all, that was what the Underworld was for, was it not? Collecting souls? I shuddered, thinking of my familiar trapped inside the darkness on the other side of the rift. Suddenly, Stella's plan made so much more sense. I mean, why call Hades in if she didn't want me to use him somehow? Gaze landing on Cassandra, I took a careful step closer, quietly enough that I didn't draw her attention away from the rift.

"My lord," she whispered over and over again, her head bowed.

I gagged a little in my mouth from her pathetic display, but somehow managed to keep my stomach from emptying on the floor. As Cassandra bowed further, I took my chance. My hands warmed with the energy of magic as I rushed toward her, my legs pumping. When I neared her, Cassandra snapped out of her daze and turned her head toward me. She was too slow. Her hands shot up, the spark of fire forming on her skin.

Not letting her finish summoning a fireball, I pressed my buzzing palms on either side of her shoulders and shoved her backward.

Cassandra's feet fumbled as she lost her balance and toppled into the rift. Her eyes rounded with fear, the darkness of the rift closing in around her as she flew further into it. Fingers stretching toward me, I watched as her fire extinguished. The witch let out a blood-curdling scream before the dark claimed her.

The Underworld had another soul.

I sank to my knees, my lungs refusing to expand. "What the heck just happened?"

"All will be clear soon, daughter," Hades said from inside the rift. "You are growing stronger. Two more moon cycles and we will reunite."

In an instant, the rift zipped closed and the pull I felt toward it disappeared. My shoulders slumped, the energy I expelled taking a toll on my already broken body. Fighting against the urge to sleep, I dragged myself toward my mother, who was barely conscious now. Cradling her into my chest, I whispered, "You're okay. We're both okay." Then I fumbled for my phone and called the sheriff, dreading having to explain what happened when he got here.

CHAPTER 24

By some small miracle, the sheriff of Orchard Hollow trusted me. At least enough that when I gave him very few details on what happened in the Prude home, he didn't cuff me immediately. After calling an ambulance for Mom— who's recovered quite nicely in the following days with the help of Cilia's healing potion— the sheriff held me back at the scene and grilled me until the sun came up.

Listening to my mother's advice, I provided him with information on what happened but kept the Sisters of the River out of it. In the end, Romero was satisfied to know that the matter was handled in a magical capacity and that none of this would come back to haunt him later.

Like me, Romero didn't enjoy not being able to arrest the person responsible for the recent deaths in town, but he agreed that the explanation they currently had for what happened was the most reliable one on paper. As far as everyone knew, Linna Cruller killed Mrs. Cevil in a heated argument over money, then drowned in a freak accident. It wasn't the truth, but it was the best we could do without letting the entire world in on our town's paranormal secrets.

I hated it.

The only thing that made it all better was knowing that the person actually responsible for the deaths was paying the price. I hadn't seen another rift since the Underworld swallowed Cassandra up like Harry swallows cookies, but I was certain she was not having one bit of fun. Served her right for what she did.

As for the Sisters, Mom assured me she would handle things on her end. I had no clue what that meant, but assumed it was best to stay in the dark. She knew the witches better than me, and despite the inner battle I pushed down; I had to trust her.

I smoothed out the wrinkles in the black dress I put on earlier and wiped the wetness from my eyes. Twirling around, I glanced in the full-length mirror in the bedroom to make sure nothing was out place before pulling my hair into a low ponytail. In my chest, my heart raced thinking about today.

"Are you almost ready, honey?" Mom called out from downstairs.

Grimacing, I forced my wild red curls into place and sighed. "Coming!"

Taking careful steps down the stairs so I don't trip over my own two feet, I met Mom in the living room. She wore a long black pantsuit with a dark-gray cardigan under a thick shawl in similar color tones. This was the least amount of color I had ever seen her put on. It broke my heart even more.

Mom's smile faltered as I approached. She reached for my hand and I let her hold it the way she used to when I was a little girl. "I'll be right there the entire time," she whispered.

"Same," I said back. "Two funerals in one day. A record for Orchard Hollow."

Sadness poured over me as I followed Mom to the front porch where Joe waited for us. I suppose it could have been worse. Linna's family moved the body to her hometown on the other side of the country or else we'd have three burials to go to. I wasn't sure how much it would have made a difference. Though Mom vaguely knew her, Linna was a stranger to me and despite her untimely end, she was keen on breaking Hades out and, according to Mom, ending life as we knew it. "Nothing good can come out of having the God of Death up here with us," she said. "Mark my words, if your father crosses over, he's bringing all his monsters with him."

It was Mrs. Cevil and Isabella's funerals that had my stomach twisted up in knots. I knew them both. Sure, not intimately, but they were a part of our town and community. They mattered to me.

Mom opened the front door and my teeth shattered as the cold wind grazed past my ankles. I instantly regretted listening to Stella and not wearing pants. Rubbing my legs together to conserve heat, I stumbled over the threshold, falling into Joe's open arms.

"Got you," he said, his breath tickling my ear.

In my belly, a million butterflies crashed into one another head first. "Thanks for coming today," I said.

"No other place I'd rather be. I didn't know Mrs. Cevil but Isabella was an acquaintance, one I don't like losing no matter what our differences were."

I recalled the warnings Joe gave me about the vampire when I first met him. None of them mattered any longer considering the situation, but I was still interested to know why he felt he needed to make them. There would be time to find out, just not today.

"I can't believe she got herself mixed up in this," Joe said.

I nodded, staying silent. After I showed the sheriff Isabella's wallet, it took him no time to track her down. Now that he knew we weren't looking for a living woman, he followed a different set of protocols, whatever that meant. All I knew was they found Isabella buried in the woods on the outskirts of town not far from a trail Cassandra frequented when she lived here ages ago. The tip came from William, surprisingly enough.

When the sheriff told me he broke the news to William about his mother, I didn't know what to expect. As it just so happened, William knew more about Cassandra's practice than she let on, likely in a misguided attempt to protect him. Her son was not as clueless as she led us to think.

"I can't believe William ratted his own mother out," I told Joe.

Stepping off the porch and onto the driveway gravel, Mom whirled around to face us. "I can," she said. "That man has no loyalty. The second Hank told him his mom was in the wind and suspected of illegal activities, he sang like a canary."

"Strange. Especially since he doesn't know the half of it."

"You mean the—" Mom made a knife stab motion in the air "—part of it?"

I nodded, slipping my arm through Joe's for

support. We walked toward Joe's car in silence, everyone marching to a slow and steady beat. As we drove to the cemetery, I caught Joe glancing at me from time to time, his face looking as though he had something to ask. I was almost one hundred percent positive it was about the surprise he returned with. Two tickets to a secluded island destination. When he presented me with the tickets, he guaranteed there was no pressure to go or to decide right away. The dates were open-ended, and the trip was there when I was ready for it, if ever.

Much to Stella Rutherford's dismay, I was yet to make a decision. Maybe after things settled down a bit.

Joe took the car around a tight bend and my body pressed into the passenger side door. I rested my forehead on the windowpane, closing my eyes for the remainder of the drive. A power nap would probably help me get some energy back though if I was being honest, I could sleep for a week after what we went through.

If only I had the luxury of time.

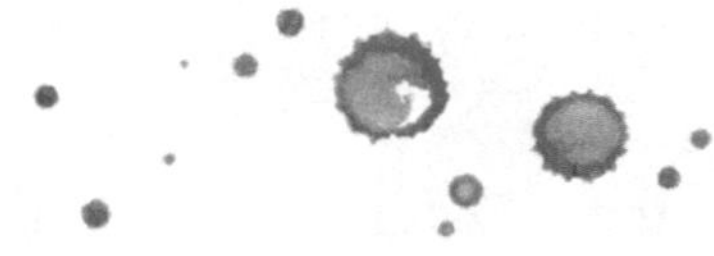

Both ceremonies were quick and tasteful and we arrived back at the farmhouse well before the sun began to set. A few storm clouds gathered, but for the most part, it was a lovely day. At least weather-wise.

Mom said that Mrs. Cevil would have said the weather turned around to make it a successful turn out for her. I laughed, picturing the bubbly old woman speaking those exact words. Somehow, I had the feeling Isabella may have held the same sentiment. In one way, the two were very much alike. Though one was a witch and one was a vampire, they both were determined, fierce women. They also both fought against the Sisters of the River which made them even better people in my books.

"About time," Stella said from the porch as the three of us returned to the house. "How did it go?"

I broke away from Joe to walk a little slower. "You could have come with us," I told the ghost.

In front of me, Mom and Joe exchanged knowing glances and went inside, leaving me alone with my familiar. It was such a relief not to hide this part of me anymore. Even though I now knew I only saw Stella Rutherford because of my ties to Hades and the Underworld, a fact that should have had me shaking in my boots. Yet it didn't. I hadn't admitted it out loud, but I felt freer somehow. As though finding out why I was different made me stronger.

The best part was I no longer had to compete with the other witches in town on account that I kind of sort of wasn't one.

"I don't do funerals," Stella said, her hands cocked on her hips.

I slanted my brows at her. "Because you're un-alive?"

"What? No! Because of all the black, Piper," the ghost huffed. "It's too dreary. Not to mention it does nothing for your complexion. You should change immediately."

"I'll do that right now," I said with a chuckle.

Starting for the door, I stopped when the ghost floated in front of me to block my path. She pressed her puffy lips tightly together, her eyes narrowing on me.

My headache started to return. "What else?"

"A couple things," Stella said. "One, the beast has returned. I caught him sneaking a ride with the mailman."

So that's how he does it, I thought. I had to hand it to Harry Houdini. He was one inventive raccoon. Crossing my arms, I studied Stella's odd expression, a worry knot forming in my throat. "What's the second thing?"

"You have a visitor."

Stella pointed to the side of the house and the

garden walkway leading to the greenhouse. My pulse sped up as I followed her gaze, wondering why she was being so cryptic. I took a step in the direction she led me and paused, looking back at her. "Who is it?"

Stella didn't answer. Rolling her eyes dramatically, she motioned for me to get going and disappeared. *Strange woman.*

Wind blew past to hurry me along and I ran up the stone path that skirted the house. When I neared the greenhouse, I skidded to a stop, the shock of what I saw sending ripples of energy down my legs. There, at the end of the path in front of the greenhouse doors, stood Isabella Beaumont. She wore a red blouse that tied with a bow at her neck and a form-hugging leather pencil skirt. My eyes traveled down her legs to the four inch, red-bottom heels she often sported around town and I could hear the clicking sound they made in my head even though the vampire wasn't moving.

My jaw gaped.

"Hello, Piper," Isabella purred. "Fancy seeing you here."

"Y-you're... b-but..." I stuttered.

The vampire rolled her shoulders. "Dead, yes, I know. How disappointing."

"I don't understand. Why can I see you?"

"Your friend with the lips mentioned something about you being able to see ghosts," Isabella said.

"Nice trick. Anyhow, I take it since I'm here, I have unfinished business. Is that how it works?"

Sweat slicked my palms despite the freezing weather. I licked my bottom lip, attempting to come up with words. "I have no idea how it works," I finally uttered.

"Wonderful."

"I mean, I have never seen anyone other than Stella," I explained. "The one with the lips, as you said. Do you know how you?" I waved an arm over her vaguely.

The vampire's features darkened. "Died? Unfortunately, it is clear as day." Her brow creased, and she tapped a talon-shaped red nail on her chin. "Do you think that's why I'm here? To help you with the Sisters of the River?"

"So you did find out about Cassandra?"

"Piper, I don't mean to be rude, but I don't know how much time I have left, and I really need you to keep up."

Dear lord of coffee, please don't let me have another Stella Rutherford on my hands. I ignored Isabella's attitude, closing some of the distance between us to show her I was all in. When I was a few feet away from the vampire ghost, she smiled approvingly and said, "There are documents in my office, notes that will explain everything I know of the coven. Cilia can let you in to look," she said. "They're in my safe. I'll give you the combination."

"Thank you. We need all the help we can get with this."

"Don't I know it," the vampire agreed. "You should know, this goes much deeper than I realized. Probably deeper than you and your mother know, too. I have contacts in the city that I shared information with. They will prove helpful to you, I believe." She looked at the house, scowling. "And tell Joe to get the stick out of his butt. The past is the past, leave it there. If you want to put an end to the coven, you're going to need my help. Time is of the essence, Piper."

Bristling, I pressed my hand to my chest, jolting when I felt the energy of my magic thrum to the surface. My breath came in quick bursts as I looked between my electric blue hands and Isabella's ghost. The vampire had no idea how right she was. Time was definitely running out and not only in the way, she thought. If I could see her, that meant the pull Hades had on me was growing. My powers were getting stronger. Somehow, I knew my father was getting stronger alongside me.

What would happen when he got too powerful to hold down?

Letting go of a slow, painful breath, I sucked in my cheeks and turned toward the farmhouse. Inside, the warm glow of the fireplace cast lively shadows on the wall as Mom and Joe moved around. I spied Stella Rutherford watching me from the window, her expression mirroring my own. Trouble was brewing on the horizon and it was up to me to stop it.

I turned away from my familiar to look at Isabella, a tired smile on my face. "Let the fun begin," I said before walking into the house, the new ghost following close behind me.

GINGERBREAD LATTE

Ingredients:

· Gingerbread simple syrup (store-bought or make your
own, see below)
· Espresso
· Milk (your preferred kind, though 3% is my favorite)
· Whipped cream
· Milk frother

Instructions:

1. Make your own Gingerbread syrup by bringing
brown sugar, granulated sugar, water, ground ginger,
and vanilla to a boil in a saucepan. Once boiled, cool
the syrup and place in an airtight container to store.
2. Pour 2 shots of espresso into your favorite mug.

3. Add 3 tablespoons of Gingerbread syrup. Mix.

4. Froth your milk and pour over the espresso and syrup mixture.

5. Add a dollop of whipped cream and top it off with a sprinkling of nutmeg.

6. Enjoy!

ABOUT THE AUTHOR

A.N. Sage is a bestselling, award-winning author of mystery and fantasy novels. She has spent most of her life waiting to meet a witch, vampire, or at least get haunted by a ghost. In between failed seances and many questionable outfit choices, she has developed a keen eye for the extra-ordinary.

A.N. spends her free time reading and binge-watching television shows in her pajamas. Currently, she resides in Toronto, Canada with her husband who is not a creature of the night and their daughter who just might be.

A.N. Sage is a Scorpio and a massive advocate of leggings for pants.

For more books and updates:
www.ansage.ca

Connect on social media:
Facebook Group:

facebook.com/groups/945090619339423/

Instagram:

instagram.com/a.n.sage/

TikTok:

tiktok.com/@ansagewrites

YouTube:

youtube.com/c/ANSageWrites

www.ingramcontent.com/pod-product-compliance
Lightning Source LLC
Chambersburg PA
CBHW050024120726
47903CB00006B/1895